The Junk Town Blues

Lyle Garford

Published by:
Lyle Garford
North Vancouver, Canada
Contact: lyle@lylegarford.com

ISBN 978-0-9936173-4-8

Cover Art by Rowan M. Davis
www.rowan-davis.co.uk

Book Design by Lyle Garford
lyle@lylegarford.com
www.lylegarford.com

First Edition 2014
Printed by CreateSpace, An Amazon.com Company
Available on Kindle and other devices

Dedication

This one is for my mother, who was a proud stick bug Mom.

Chapter One

The two young wolves paused to sniff at the wind in wary silence. Until now they had been padding along soft and quiet, trying to stay undetected as long as possible. Travelling in the low undergrowth of the forest had worked well to this point, keeping them hidden longer than they thought possible. With a quick look at each other they congratulated themselves on getting this close to the border of Junk Town without the alarm being raised.

"And they thought we couldn't do it," said the older of the two wolves. "We won't be going hungry tonight, buddy."

"I think we should grab as much as we can carry and have a feast right in front of the pack," replied the other with an evil grin.

Neither would admit a little worm of doubt ate at both of them, though. The older wolves in their pack were all wary of Junk Town, far too much in the opinion of the two young wolves. Home to a host of pet animals abandoned by humans, Junk Town was still a tempting target for hungry predators. But their pack leader Scar had seen the young wolves bravery and desire, so he gave them permission to try an attack.

They hadn't expected to get his approval. Although surprised and a bit puzzled at Scar's support, the two young and aggressive wolves spent little time wondering about it and continued to be scornful in private of the older wolves they thought were too timid. Bringing some fresh prey back from Junk Town was the surest way to prove it.

But doubt still ate at them. What if the older wolves were right?

The older lead wolf shrugged off his doubts. "Come on, let's get a little closer if we can before we rush them."

Peering with hungry eyes through the thinning brush it was clear staying concealed couldn't last much longer. Once past the old fence on the border the fringe of trees and brush surrounding the edges of Junk Town was disappearing, with only a few trees and shrubs to provide cover from this point on. As they got even closer they stopped worrying about losing their cover, however. Of much more interest was the sight of prey, so many that the hungry wolves began salivating in anticipation.

"Look over there, Slash!" said the lead wolf.

In the distance was a strange collection of little homes put together from a crazy assortment of materials stretching all the way from a beat up old trailer at one end of the property to a little barn standing alone at the other end. It was like someone had taken a dozen giant jigsaw puzzles, jumbled them up at random, and put it all back together with a basic sense of order. A deep stream cut through the heart of Junk Town, complete with a few little bridges to help cross over. However, the inhabitants of Junk Town were what interested the wolves.

A wide assortment of creatures bustled about with purpose everywhere they went. Dogs, cats, and rats were plentiful, and best of all, there was a whole host of plump, tasty looking rabbits! Several were laboring in the fields surrounding Junk

Town, tending to crops of carrots and lettuce just beginning to sprout in the spring sunshine.

"They're going to be so jealous when we bring back a bunch of these rabbits. Look at how fat they are!" said Slash, salivating even more at the prospect. Baring his fangs in a savage grin he nodded in silence in the direction of the nearest field filled with rabbit workers. "This is as close as we're going to get without being seen. Are you ready?"

The other wolf grinned and nodded in reply. Bursting from their cover as one the wolves barreled forward in a headlong rush.

The rabbits at work in the field were focused on their work and had no idea of the dire threat coming their way. The confidence of the attackers soared ever higher the closer they got without their presence being detected. Then, sensing something wrong, a rabbit twitched alert and looked around. Glancing in their direction he froze for a brief moment in shock before sounding the alarm. The field rabbits twitched in fear as they grasped the danger and they scattered in all directions running hard to escape.

The need for stealth was gone, replaced by the joy of the hunt. "Get them, Slash!" howled the lead wolf.

His howl of victory changed almost instantly to a howl of surprise. A thin, cleverly hidden trip wire strung across his path made him stumble as the wire triggered the trap with a loud snap. The two wolves were shocked as they crashed together and were abruptly pulled off their feet. Struggling to understand what was happening, they both howled in frustration and fear, but their struggles got them nowhere. The big net swinging wildly back and forth in the air held the two wolves fast.

The rabbit engineers of Junk Town had laid their trap well. A big old fishing net salvaged from the junkyard and camouflaged on the ground held the two struggling wolves firm in its grasp. Thoughts of trying to chew through the net were immediately dismissed by the frustrated wolves, as the netting was far too thick.

Still howling in frustration and fear, there was little they could do but await their fate. A small, wary crowd of Junk Town animals soon gathered to gawk at the captured wolves. Many hung back, on edge and ready to run at a moments notice. Being this close to wolves, even ones thoroughly trapped like these, was a frightening thought for many.

A small group of the bolder young rats were the exception. "Look at these idiots!" laughed one of them, making the wolves snarl in frustration. Slash managed to get a paw through one of the rings in the net and began slashing the air wildly in their direction.

"Stop that, you fool!" shouted his partner. "You're making me sick from all this motion."

The sick look on his face just made the rats laugh even louder as the net wildly swayed back and forth. They moved aside though, still laughing, as two new animals made their way through to the front of the crowd. The wolves could see the rest of the watching animals were respectful of the newcomers and were clearly expecting them to take action.

The two animals seemed an odd pair on the surface. The first was a rabbit, clearly a leader bearing the quiet air of command. Today he seemed curious and puzzled as he focused on the still trapped wolves swaying in the net in front of him.

The other was a strange looking bug, quite a bit smaller than his partner. But like all stick bugs, he had a wiry strength that wasn't apparent at first. Glaring at the trapped wolves, the stick bug shook his head in frustration and turned to his partner.

"Well, that's the third time this month and the month isn't even half over, Twitch. What is it with them, anyway? They came after us only twice in all of the last month. You think they're getting more active because it's spring?"

Twitch the rabbit shrugged. "Could be, Sticks. Mind you, those two attacks last month were towards the end, weren't they? At least they aren't getting any smarter. Our traps have got them every time."

"Huh," replied Sticks, a concerned look growing on his face. "These two look like young rookies. I'm just not sure why they're here so soon. I think they're either just rogues that couldn't wait for Scar to stir himself to action again or maybe this is part of some larger plot on the part of Scar."

"A plot? To do what? You think he's that smart, Sticks?"

"Don't know. We beat him before, but it might just be he's adapting. Or maybe he's just plotting something different. I don't like this."

That thought gave both of them pause, bringing back memories from the year before. Sticks and his family were grateful to make a new home for themselves in Junk Town after being unceremoniously abandoned in the forest by their former owner just as winter was approaching. The memory of the shocking loss of his father and grandfather in a flood during their struggle to reach Junk Town had faded, but was still painful.

The burden of leading the family fell to Sticks. They soon found they liked Junk Town and its inhabitants, but attacks by predators meant life was not easy. With the help of the old human and Stuff the bear the predators had been kept at bay. The predator's fortunes changed when Stuff was captured and taken away by humans. Worse, soon after that the old human passed away.

Sticks rose to the challenge. Leading the Junk Town animals in a desperate defense of their home against a massive combined attack from the wolves and crows, Sticks had handed their enemies a crushing defeat.

For the first few months after as fall changed to winter there were no attacks, but then they began again. Twitch and his engineer rabbits worked overtime to construct a new series of defenses and traps like the one that caught the two wolves still snarling at them in frustration. So far, at least, the defenses had worked.

This time Sticks was reacting differently though, and Twitch looked hard at Sticks. "You know, I've been around you long enough now I can tell when you've got something on your mind. Come on, out with it. What's up?"

"Okay, you got me," said Sticks, with deliberate slowness, lowering his voice so the two wolves couldn't hear him. "I'd like to think they don't know what they're doing, but that would presume too much. So just keep looking at these two idiots for the moment, because I don't want to give away the game. There's a crow hidden in those trees off to our right watching all of this. He's being very careful to ensure he isn't seen and I don't think it's a coincidence he's there. I was lucky to spot him out of the corner of my eye when he shifted his position. So I figure we have to err on the safe side and assume this is part of a larger plan."

"Hmm, yes, I agree," replied Twitch. "So where do we go from here?"

"We give that some thought and talk it over later."

"Sure. What do you want to do with these two?"

Smiling, Sticks raised his voice so the wolves could hear him again. "Well, we could round up everyone and shove them out of town with the pointy end of our spears, but Stuff is coming by this evening to hang out at the fire with us. I'm sure he'd be happy to explain to these two fools why it's a bad idea to come after us."

Twitch laughed as the two wolves cringed at the mention of Stuff. The fearsome young bear had wandered into Junk Town with an injured paw the year before and the old human had helped to heal it. Orphaned by hunters, he had adopted Junk Town and it's residents as his new family. The wolves had soon learned it was a bad mistake to come after any of the residents while he was around.

That was before he was captured and tagged by animal control officers because they thought he was a 'garbage bear', too used to looking for food in garbage cans. Stuff had found himself hauled off into the deep forest and released. After weary days of travelling he got back just in time to help defeat the predators in the Battle of Junk Town. Since then he had mostly kept a wary distance from Junk Town. If the humans caught him near the city again he would be put down.

With the tag the humans had attached to his ear still in place there was no other choice. Twitch and his rabbit engineers had tried to get it off without injuring the bear several times, but it had so far defeated every attempt. This meant Stuff was forced to vary his visits to Junk Town with an irregular schedule and to not stay for very long when he did.

"Ah," said Twitch, after he'd stopped laughing at the wolves. "I didn't know Stuff was coming by tonight, but I'm glad he is. I'm told my engineers have dreamed up another way to get that thing off of him, so maybe they can try it tonight."

"Excellent. And in the meantime, these two can just hang here and consider the error of their ways. But what do you think? Will that net hold them that long?"

"Oh yes," replied Twitch. "They made sure the nets were as strong as could be."

Slash, more aggressive than the other wolf and still angry at being trapped, had been growling and trying once again to get a paw far enough out of the net to claw at the two animals in front of him. Sticks smiled and addressed the wolf directly.

"Hey, ugly. Yeah, that's you. Tell your boss Scar he's wasting his time. As for you two, don't come back. We may not be so nice next time."

Turning, both animals left as the two wolves growled in frustration, still swaying back and forth in the net from their struggles.

***

Now that warmer spring weather had come a big fire wasn't needed, but everyone enjoyed watching the endless shapes of the flames shift as they fought back the night. The crowd gathered that night had fed well on their stored supplies, but many were looking forward to having fresh crops as the year wore on. For the most part it was a content and happy group around the fire.

Stuff the bear had indeed appeared for dinner as promised. His presence immediately cheered everyone and it wasn't just because he brought guaranteed safety from attack. The Junk Town animals genuinely enjoyed the cheerful young bear and they all knew he felt the same way about them.

When told about the two wolves still hanging trapped in the net he had growled deep in his throat and turned to find them. Sticks stopped him briefly and smiled. "Just the usual, Stuff. No need to beat them up."

"Leave it to me," growled the bear over his shoulder as he stalked over to them. A large crowd of the Junk Town children eager to watch their enemies humbled followed along.

The wolves in the net cringed and tried to shrink away seeing the big bear coming to stand before them. Stuff simply glared at them for a long minute before putting his snout close the net. No one could hear what he said, but the hard, menacing undertone in his voice was crystal clear.

With sudden, stunning speed the bear cut open a large chunk of the net holding the wolves fast. The wolves howled in fear and terror as they crashed hard to the ground in front of Stuff. Their howls were cut short as Stuff roared in anger and swatted both of them hard.

The Junk Town children rolled on the ground laughing as the two wolves stumbled and struggled to get out of the net still tangling them. Both got free at the same time and ran hard for the safety of the trees. Realizing Stuff wasn't chasing them the older wolf paused at the tree line and looked back. Stuff just glared back at him and growled. The wolf bared his fangs in a grim, mocking smile and disappeared into the woods.

Back at the fire several animals thanked Stuff for dealing with the wolves. Stuff gave them a sad smile in return.

"What's wrong, Stuff?" asked one of the rabbits sitting by the fire.

The bear took a moment to reply, sitting down beside the rabbit and making himself comfortable. "Ah, I'm just wishing I could be here to help more. I miss all you guys and it feels personal every time you get attacked. You wouldn't need to live in fear or have to put up all these defenses and traps if I could stay here with you."

"Well, I have news, Stuff," said Twitch. "The boys want to have another go at getting that tag off you tonight. With any luck you'll be able to rejoin us."

"That would be great Twitch!" replied Stuff, a hopeful look on his face. "I'm ready whenever they are."

Several animals voiced their support and hope it would work, but Sticks was noticeably quiet. Stick's sister Leaf knew him well and could see he had something on his mind. "What are you thinking, dear brother? Come on, I can see you've got something to say."

Sticks grimaced as he saw many animals turn to hear his response. "Yeah," he finally replied. "I'd prefer I had something positive to say about this, though. I'm afraid I don't."

"What do you mean?"

"Ah, well, I've been thinking about this for some time. We've all been focused on finding a way to get this tag off his ear, right?"

Seeing nods from the crowd of animals around the fire he continued. "We all figured we'd be safe once and for all if that happened and Stuff could live here again with us. And yes, that would be great for all of us that need protection. What about Stuff, though? The reason he got hauled away is Junk Town is too close to the city and the humans are afraid of him. I don't know, I guess I'm just afraid it could happen again. And I don't know about any of you, but I don't want to watch my friend Stuff get hauled off in a cage again."

The look of gloom appearing on the faces of the animals as the implications of what he'd said sunk in told him he was right. Several of the animals groaned and nodded in agreement.

Stuff put on a brave face. "I'm willing to take that risk. With the junk yard closed there aren't any humans coming around here any more."

"That's true, Stuff, but how long will that last?" replied Sticks. "I don't know, I just can't see the humans leaving this place the way it is. Maybe someone will move in and take over the business? Who knows?"

"Wow," said Leaf. "You're just full of cheery thoughts tonight, aren't you?"

Sticks grimaced and shrugged his shoulders. Finally forcing a smile, he looked around at the gathered animals. "Sorry. You asked. Well, there's not much we can do about this tonight. Let's eat."

Chapter Two

Conversation was subdued as the hungry animals finished dinner and cleaned up. Many had eaten their meals in thoughtful silence, still digesting what Sticks had said.

A few faces grew hopeful looks as the rabbit engineers used the light of the fire torches around the clearing to set about once again trying to get the tag off Stuff's ear. After several minutes of muttered discussion and tinkering with the tag the two rabbits leading the attempt groaned loudly and threw up their hands in disgust.

Twitch walked over to see them and spent several more minutes in deep discussion before returning to the rest of the waiting animals. Seeing they expected a report, he could only shrug. "Sorry everyone, this obviously didn't work either. The problem is whatever this tag is made of. It's some kind of real hard, strong metal that's beating every attempt to break or cut it off without mangling poor Stuff's ear in the process. Well, we're going to keep trying. Still a few more ideas to try out so don't give up hope."

The hopeful faces fell as fast as they had appeared and a few animals sighed aloud. A rushing sound of wings coming closer proved a welcome distraction. With his usual flourish, Rawk the parrot made a grand entrance by circling the crowd twice and finally landing in their midst by the fire.

Rawk was his usual wild, colorful self. As if his multi colored feathers weren't enough today he wore a yellow blazer jacket with blue flowers on it together with a matching hat.

"Hey, what's with the long faces around here? I'm back now, its time to smile!" laughed the parrot. Rawk took his role as chief entertainer in Junk Town seriously. Everyone knew frowns were banned in his presence.

"I would've been back sooner, but I was off in an area close to the mountains that I haven't been to before. I met a whole bunch of different animals so it kept me away longer. I found a real interesting place right at the end, too, but I was tired so I have to go back and check it out some more later."

Looking around, he could see a few in the audience warming to his presence with little smiles, but most were still feeling gloomy. Putting his hands on his sides he took on a mocking, stern look. "Okay, come on, here. If I don't get some smiles out of this terribly serious bunch soon I'm going to make you all put on clown suits and do one of my Rawk special line dances as punishment."

That brought a few more smiles to the faces, but many seemed wistful. "Right, that's it," huffed the parrot, still looking stern. "Who's responsible for all this grumpiness around here? Time to get out the chicken hat."

Several animals immediately laughed and pointed at Sticks, who groaned and hung his head.

"You? Honestly, you know better," said Rawk before flying off.

Returning from the old human's trailer where Rawk still lived he flew back with a hat shaped in the form of a chicken's head. "You know the new rule around here, Sticks. If you're going to insist on making everyone grouchy you'll have to do it with the chicken hat on."

Planting it on the stick bug's head Rawk stepped back to admire the result. "Oh, yeah, that's you, Mr. Mayor. Hey, maybe we should make this your official badge of office! You could wear it every night!"

Sticks glared at the parrot as the crowd howled with laughter. "Yeah, I don't think so, Rawk. You might be having to find a new Mayor if you do that."

"Okay," replied Rawk. "So what's this grumpiness all about here, anyway? You're making my job difficult. It's even harder getting this bunch to laugh when they're in a bad mood."

Sticks explained what he'd talked about earlier and how the attempt to free Stuff from the tag had failed, adding to the worried mood of the Junk Town animals.

"Huh," said the parrot. "Sorry, I don't get it. It's been like this with Stuff for a long time now. It'd be great to have him around all the time, but he can still visit. So why are you sharing your grumpiness with everyone?"

Sticks grimaced and sighed, turning to Twitch with a questioning look. Twitch shrugged and nodded in silent agreement.

"Right, well, since I'm doomed to wearing this chicken hat for tonight I may as well confess. Twitch and I have been worried for a while about what's been happening. You may have noticed the wolves have been getting more active lately. We don't know if it's because it's spring or what, but their attacks have increased. Our rabbit engineer friends have outwitted them so far with the traps, but we're concerned they're plotting something much bigger."

"What makes you think that?" asked Sniff the rat.

"The sudden increase in the number of attempts for starters. Plus, today we saw a crow hidden in the trees watching what happened. I think he was spying on us."

"So there's a crow too scared of us to come out and take us on," grumbled Sniff. "Big deal. Like you said, we've done pretty well to this point."

"Well, yes, but I think that's the problem. I'm beginning to see a pattern in these attacks. They've all been one or two wolves at a time and they've all been young rookies. We haven't even seen these two particular wolves before so they know nothing about Junk Town and us. See, I think Scar may not be as dumb as we thought. I think he's sending his least experienced wolves to stumble headlong into whatever traps we've laid for them. He's testing our defenses so he can plan a better, bigger attack on us. And the hidden crow watching it all today was maybe Scar's buddy Spike or one of his crow followers with the job of reporting back."

"Reporting what, Mr. Mayor? Why is that a concern?" asked one of the older rabbit children, poking his head up through the crowd to be seen.

"Ah, well. You wouldn't maybe have been told, but you might as well know. When danger appears you know you've been given a specific hiding place to go to, right? Well, your parents and the rest of us adults all have specific jobs to do when this happens, too. See, we have other defenses we haven't had to use yet in case they get past the traps we've set on our borders. Twitch and I don't think the crow we saw today was concerned at all about what happened to the two wolves. I think he was really there to watch us and see what we did and where we went when trouble appeared, hoping to see what we had in store for them so they could be prepared to counter it."

The watching crowd of animals was silent for a few moments as they digested everything Sticks had said, until Sniff the rat broke the silence once again. "Yeah, well, I say bring it on. Let them come after us, we clobbered them once and we can do it again."

"Hmm, well, there's one other thing to consider," replied Sticks. "Like I said, we haven't seen these two idiots we caught today before, same as all of the others we've encountered in the last little while. Twitch and I have compared notes on this and we're sure of that, we both have real clear memories of what the wolves that attacked us last year looked like. So the real problem could be maybe Scar is recruiting new wolves for his pack. And it could be his crow buddy Spike is perhaps adding to his flock too. I think the plan is to get past our defenses by spying them out and then overwhelming us with sheer numbers."

Silence descended on the crowd once again and stayed this time. Even Rawk was deep in thought.

A distant crash broke the silence and everyone turned to find the source. The sound had come from the far border of Junk Town near the forest. A loud howl of pain and a muffled thrashing sound quickly followed.

Twitch and several of his rabbits looked at each other. "That's another one of our traps, I think," said Twitch.

Several animals got up and headed in the direction of the sound. Stuff the bear immediately took the lead, already rumbling his displeasure at the disturbance.

"Leave this to us, Twitch," said the bear as he left. "If those same two fools have come back they're going to pay. They may not have thought I was serious when I told them I could use some nice wolf fur rugs for my den."

The remaining animals settled back to their seats and stared in silence at the fire. The sounds of a distant commotion soon filled the air, followed once again by silence.

Eventually the defenders returned to the fire and Stuff reported to Sticks. "It was a lone wolf this time and he wasn't one of the two you caught earlier, lucky for him. He broke a leg falling into a hidden pit our rabbit friends had built to trap fools like him. I sent him on his way without beating him up after the rabbits put a splint on him and gave him a little crutch so he could hobble away. He's already paying the price for trying to get us. Of course, before he left I explained I would personally break the rest of his legs if he ever comes back here again."

One of the rabbit engineers that had accompanied Stuff raised a paw for attention. "Twitch? I kept an eye out like you said and you were right. There were two crows hiding this time, watching the whole thing. I tried to make sure they didn't know I'd seen them. As for the wolf I'm pretty sure we haven't seen him before either."

Another deep silence descended and worried looks appeared once again on the faces of the animals around the fire. Sticks's twin sister Leaf finally spoke up, stepping to the front of the crowd to speak. "Right, well, it seems pretty clear you two are right and we have a problem again. So, Mr. Mayor, what are you planning to do about it?"

"Uh, well, I don't know. We've only just reached the point where we've realized this is likely what's happening. I haven't given any thought to dealing with it. Twitch? What about you?"

"The same," replied the rabbit. "I can get my crew to dream up even more nasty surprises if need be, I guess. But I think you're right to be concerned, especially if they've already been spying on us and know what we've been up to."

"Not good enough, Mr. Mayor," laughed Leaf. "We've come to expect miracles you know. We'll have to elect somebody like Rawk for our Mayor if you don't get your act together."

"Sorry," smiled Rawk. "Being the number one entertainer around here is plenty for me, thanks. But I think our Mayor's counselors need to help out here. If no one else has a suggestion I do." Looking around, Rawk could see he had the crowd's attention, so he continued. "Well, I'm thinking if our problem is we have too many attackers, maybe we need more defenders. Why don't we do some recruiting, just like Scar?"

Several faces lit up as they considered the possibility. Checkers, the oldest of the dogs living in Junk Town, finally broke the silence. "What, this place isn't crowded enough? Besides, who'd want to come and live in a place under threat of constant attack?"

Sniff the rat just laughed. "Better stop being so cheerful or Rawk is going to take the chicken hat from Sticks and make you wear it. Besides, you came to live here, didn't you?" Sniff smiled as Checkers scowled in his direction and turned to the rest of the watching animals. "Actually, I think that idea has potential. There's plenty of room around here, despite what he says. Rawk, didn't you say something earlier about meeting some new animals?"

"Yes, well, that's what gave me the idea. There seems to be no shortage of abandoned animals out there." Turning to Sticks and Leaf, he gave them a huge grin. "Some of them you might be particularly interested in."

Sticks and Leaf looked at each other and then back at the parrot, both replying at the same time. "What?"

The parrot just kept grinning, waiting for them to think it through. Leaf was the first to realize Rawk could only be talking about one thing. "I'll bet you found more stick bugs! You did, didn't you?" she cried, as Rawk smiled and nodded agreement. "Oh, Sticks, we have to invite them to come here!"

"Well, hang on, let's hear some more, shall we? Maybe they're happy where they are? Tell us more, Rawk."

"Yes, indeed, I met a little group of stick bugs although I almost missed them as I flew by. You guys are really good at hiding yourselves! I know what to watch for now for courtesy of being around all of you, but without that practice I'd never have seen them. So, yes, they were abandoned like you. There are eight of them and they've made a little home for themselves, but I don't think they've been as successful at defending themselves. They seemed very interested in Junk Town." Turning, the parrot looked deliberately at Checkers. "And yes, I did make it clear we get attacked here too."

"So what's happening, Rawk?" asked Leaf. "Are they coming here?"

"Yes, indeed, I was pretty sure everyone would be happy to have a few more stick bugs around so I took the liberty of inviting them. Besides, you can never have too large an audience! They'll probably be a couple of days getting here as I was pretty far away when I found them."

The animals crowded about the fire all began speaking at once. Sticks and Twitch spent a few minutes deep in conversation and then gradually attempted to get everyone's attention. When the buzz of conversation finally died away, Sticks smiled at Rawk.

"You never fail to come through for us, Rawk, and it looks like you've done it again." Sticks looked around and addressed the crowd directly. "Well, everyone? Looks like we're going to have some new residents. What about inviting a whole bunch more?"

The ensuing roar made Sticks smile. The simple solution of growing Junk Town to a size too big to be overcome had grabbed the imaginations of the animals. Sticks waved for attention once more and waited for the conversations to die down as he turned to speak to Rawk.

"So you've got this rolling by inviting our stick bug cousins. Who else did you invite?"

"Well, no one, but I told them all about it and they seemed interested. After I invited the stick bugs I figured I'd better check in with all of you before I got out of control. It wasn't huge numbers, if that's what you're wondering. A few more dogs and cats mostly. Twitch, I found a few more rabbits, too. Ah, and there was one interesting abandoned animal. Any of you ever seen a potbellied pig?"

"A pig?" asked Leaf. "Are you serious? Someone had a pig as a pet and abandoned them?"

"Apparently. I didn't get a lot of details from him. I almost missed him too. Fortunately he stuck his head out of his den just as I flew by and it seemed so weird to see a pig in the forest I just had to stop."

"Right, well," mused Sticks, looking thoughtful and turning to the crowd once again. "Okay, everyone, so I'm thinking we put out a general call as far and wide as possible. We extend an invitation to anyone and everyone that wants to join us. Safety in numbers, that's the message. Thing is, we could get just about anyone or anything, for that matter, taking us up on the offer.

Twitch and I talked, there is room to expand around the old human's trailer and we can grow our defensive traps as Junk Town grows. Best of all, if this works our friend Stuff won't have to worry about our safety so much and put himself at risk by coming here too often. So are we okay with the thought of having a whole bunch more neighbors? Maybe even potbellied pigs?"

The watching animals were all silent for a few moments, looking around at each other. One by one, though, they all smiled and nodded agreement.

Leaf broke the silence once again. "Can I make a suggestion? Obviously Rawk knows of a few animals already we can invite here and will likely find some more. But why should we leave all that on his shoulders? He can't be everywhere at once. I think we should take advantage of some of our other friends to help out too."

"Yes, I agree," said Sticks. "If we put a message out through the forest birds Rawk knows that would help. Wally can maybe talk our squirrel soccer friends into doing the same. It won't take long to get the message out. So let's do it."

Sniff the rat stepped to the front of the crowd and looked deliberately at Rawk as everyone nodded agreement once again. "I guess you know I don't hand out compliments very often. That means you should enjoy this and not get used to it." Turning, Sniff laughed and addressed the crowd. "The bird deserves a round of applause, don't you think?"

The crowd roared, leaping to their feet as they clapped long and hard. Rawk laughed along with them and took a deep bow. "I'll take whatever applause I can get, Sniff!"

As it finally died down, Sticks stepped forward grinning and looked at Rawk. "We've noticed that, Rawk. So now that everyone's happy and smiling again, can I please take this silly hat off?"

Chapter Three

The following days flew by, full of activity resulting from a steady parade of newcomers arriving in Junk Town.

The potbellied pig Rawk had found, whose name was Peter, was one of the first to arrive late the next day. Everyone was surprised at how soon he had come until he explained how lonely he had been. Being a social animal used to being part of a herd he had been very lonely on his own in the forest. Peter quickly set about meeting everyone and building a little shelter for himself close to the stream. Everyone was puzzled by how eager he was to build there until they realized it was important so he wouldn't have far to haul water for the little hollowed out spot he used to make a puddle to lie in on the really hot days.

The Junk Town animals had no trouble drawing out his story. At his first evening around the fire he was only too happy to talk. "I grew up on a little farm with a bunch of other pigs just like me. It was great until the owner sold me. It turns out he was raising us to sell as pets because for a while it was fashionable for humans to have a potbellied pig as a pet. I was dumped in the forest after about six months because the owner's children got tired of me. I guess they also thought I was too much work to care for and I wasn't happy. To be fair, I was really missing my friends in the herd so I was probably too grouchy for them."

The Junk Town animals were happy to welcome him. Looking thoughtful, one of the rabbit children spoke up. "Peter? Maybe we can be your herd now?"

Peter gave a bright smile and almost did a dance in response. "That's exactly what I'm hoping!"

He wasn't the only unusual animal to arrive on their doorstep. Several Junk Town animals were now keeping a wary, constant watch on the trees for crows spying on them, but one day they found something very different. A little family of monkeys Rawk had invited was spotted high in the trees, watching the bustle of activity that was daily life in Junk Town. Realizing they'd been seen brought them into the open, but they remained wary until Rawk made an appearance and coaxed them down to have dinner around the fire that night.

The parent monkeys were Buster and Betty. Two little ones with big eyes clung close to Mom for the first while, but that didn't last long. They were soon leaping and rushing about, climbing on everything and everyone. All of the Junk Town animals were approached with playful curiosity. Wally, the resident Australian stick bug, made friends with them immediately.

Laughing, he danced with them by the fire. "Hello, mates! We're going to have to keep an eye on you two scamps, aren't we? Look at how quick and shifty they are. Hey, do any of you play soccer by any chance?" he added, looking with sudden interest at the two parent monkeys.

"Never heard of it," replied Buster, after a puzzled glance at his wife. "Our humans never let us out at all, until they dumped us in the forest."

"Not to worry, mate," said Wally with a big grin. "I've got a feeling you're going to like this. The squirrel soccer team won't know what hit them!"

***

The new stick bugs Rawk had found finally arrived the next day. Twitch, Sticks, and Leaf were all standing in the newest part of Junk Town watching the ground being cleared to make way for some new animal homes. A commotion in the distance caught their attention and they soon realized one of the border guard rats was escorting the newcomers through the maze of traps set by the engineer rabbits.

As they came closer the guard rat detoured over to where they were waiting to introduce them. Both Sticks and Wally's jaws dropped when they saw the female stick bug walking beside the rat.

"Whoa, mate. She's a looker," said Wally. "Absolutely stunning, in ...oww!"

Leaf scowled at Wally, having elbowed her future husband hard in the stomach to get his attention. "Yes, she is a 'looker', isn't she?"

"Well, she's not as good looking as you, my love," said Wally with haste. Looking as repentant as he could, Wally gave her a hopeful smile.

"Oh, stop it, you oaf," she replied, rolling her eyes, as the party of newcomers stopped in front of them. As Rawk had said there were eight of them, six adult males and females, and two little ones that clung close to one of the older females. Two of the adult stick bugs were very frail and old. The good looking younger of the two females looked expectantly at the three stick bugs, waiting for someone to speak.

Leaf glared at Sticks, still standing with a stunned look on his face, as the silence grew embarrassing. "What, you too?" she said with a groan.

"Ignore these two fools, please," said Leaf, giving the newcomers an exasperated look as she reached out to shake their hands. "Welcome to Junk Town! Must say I never thought we'd come across more stick bugs out here. I'm Leaf."

"Thank you! I'm Windy," replied the female, introducing the others with her. "We're glad to be here." A look of relief stole across her face and everyone could see she and the others were almost exhausted. "It was a long, hard march to get here. We were attacked three times along the way. But I feel a little safer already. So who do we see about settling in here?"

Glaring at her brother, Leaf replied before Sticks could speak. "Well, if my idiot brother here has recovered himself, you can talk to him. Who knows why, but we did elect him Mayor of Junk Town, after all."

"Uh...right," stammered Sticks, staring now at the somewhat older, big male stick bug, whose name was Twiggs, standing protectively near the female before turning back to Windy. "Yes. It's very nice to meet you all. Sure, we'll find somewhere temporary for you tonight, maybe the old barn will do. We're getting started on building some more homes here as you can see, but we need a little more time."

"Okay, well, thank you Mr., uh... Mayor. We don't need much."

"When he's not a dummy without the manners to introduce himself his name is Sticks," said Leaf. "And in case you were wondering, this tongue tied fool beside me is Wally, my future husband." Rolling her eyes in mock frustration once again, she laughed. "I know. I don't know what I was thinking."

Wally just gave her a winning smile and looked at the newcomers. "G'day mates, and yes, I'm an Aussie stick bug, since I know you were wondering."

"Huh," said Tracy, the slightly older female stick bug with the two awestruck little stick bugs still clinging to her. "Yes, I think we were all curious."

Windy smiled. "Well, I guess we have lots to learn here. Can we do that after we get settled in and rest a bit?"

***

The list of things to do seemed endless for the next several days. A steady stream of newcomers appeared almost daily, creating what seemed an endless series of demands on the residents of Junk Town. Temporary homes had to be found while new ones were being built. New defenses had to be constructed for the changed borders and the old traps dismantled and moved.

For the newcomers to Junk Town it was all very strange and different as they wandered around looking dazed, trying to find their way about. They were awestruck at the castle defenses the Junk Town animals had built. Over the winter the engineers had been hard at work, repairing damage from The Battle of Junk Town.

They hadn't stopped with just doing repairs, though. Two new castles had been built at strategic locations and all of them had been modified to add a strange looking tower to each. They were a puzzling addition to Junk Town, looming over the landscape as they did. The engineers had covered the towers with old plastic panels to conceal what was behind them.

Twitch gave the new stick bugs a mysterious smile when they asked what they were for. "Just another little surprise we've put together. You'll be fully briefed after you're settled in."

A little team of engineers were assigned to help the new stick bugs build a little residence for themselves close to where the rest of the stick bugs already lived. With a frenzy of effort the job hadn't taken long. The grateful elder stick bugs gave every one of the rabbit engineers a big hug of thanks when they saw the final result.

With that done everyone could then be taught where both the new and old traps were and be assigned a role in the defense of Junk Town. For the newcomers learning and understanding the simple fact they even had a role in a coordinated defense seemed very strange.

A coordinated defense had not been put together overnight or come easily. After their stunning victory over the wolves and crows last fall Sticks and Twitch agreed they had to stay vigilant. Both knew that being overconfident because of their total victory was the real danger to them all.

To ease this risk they'd spent considerable effort convincing the Junk Town animals of the need to plan a defense. So in addition to creating a series of traps and defensive positions, they'd eventually worked out through trial and error a defensive strategy that meant individual animals needed to know exactly what their job was when they were attacked. The problem Sticks and Twitch now faced was the end result of adding more animals to their plans, changing the roles of some of the animals, and changing the layout of their defenses. The outcome was close to mass confusion.

The next attack came at the worst possible time, while the confusion was still widespread and the defenses still under construction. Four wolves came in a howling rush early one morning, this time approaching from the clearing in front of the old human's trailer. Sticks and Twitch both agreed later it was likely no coincidence that this was the area they were expanding their borders and the new defenses were still weak. Making the confusion complete was the wolves were chasing a group of rats running as hard as they could for the safety of Junk Town.

Despite the muddle the Junk Town animals soon leapt to the defense. One of the wolves grabbed a border guard rat that had bravely sounded the alarm and then stood his ground trying to help the rats being chased. One of the other wolves began chasing a group of three engineer rabbits that had been working on building new homes. The other two continued at full speed after the fleeing rats, just now reaching the rest of the stunned Junk Town animals.

The defenders rallied around Sticks, who immediately led a tightly bunched band of defenders to the attack. "Spear Groups One and Two! Focus on helping the rat and the rabbits. Slingshot Groups! Fire when ready at those other two!"

Rushing forward the groups did as ordered, jabbing hard at the wolf chasing the rabbits while the other group with spears being led by Sticks thrust from all directions at the wolf with the rat in his jaws, trying to convince him to free his victim. Both wolves tried to slash back at the defenders with their claws, but the long spears of the Junk Town animals mostly kept them at bay. The defenders all now carried lightweight shields the engineer rabbits had built for them and these saved several animals from being slashed when the wolves did get past the spears. However, it was a hail of sharp rocks from the slingshot groups that finally stopped both of the remaining wolves in their tracks.

The sound of cawing laughter from above froze the defenders and they turned as one to find the source. Two crows, seeing how easily the wolves had penetrated the defense decided to stop their spying and join the fight. A group of rabbit children that had been passing by when the fight began became the target. Their screams were pitiful as they tried dodging the claws and sharp beaks of the birds.

"Slingshot Group Two!" screamed Sticks. "The crows are yours!" Immediately, one of the

groups of defenders with slingshots detached itself
from the fight with the wolves and began firing at
the crows. The birds reacted by flying low and
chasing after the little rabbits, meaning the shooters
didn't have a clear shot. The wolves, meanwhile,
suddenly had an easier time chasing their prey
because the defense was now fragmented.
Although more Junk Town animals were
responding to the calls for help, the battle was not
going well.

The newcomers helped turn the tide. With
an angry squeal Peter the pig barreled into the wolf
still clutching the now unconscious rat in his jaws,
knocking the wolf off his feet and making him drop
his prey. "Leave my herd alone," snarled the pig as
he bared his teeth.

The wolf was shocked that he'd been taken
down, but he didn't stay that way for long. "What?
A pig that thinks he can take me on? Well, lets see
how good you are, piggy. I'll bet you'd be real good
eating for dinner tonight." With a snarl of his own
the wolf came on in a frightening rush.

The wolf had expected the pig to run, as so
many other animals did when charged. Peter did
the exact opposite, charging straight at the wolf
with power and speed. The two came together in a
monumental, crashing blur of fangs and claws. The
pig, being about as large as a medium sized dog, but
much heavier, bowled into the chest of the wolf
with stunning force. Both crashed to the ground
for a moment, trying to recover their senses.

Realizing the pig wasn't backing down, the
wolf began to circle and look for an opening. Peter
responded with quick, short rushes at the wolf,

trying to hurt the wolf with hard head butts and biting wherever he could. Peter knew he had a chance if he could keep himself directly facing the attacking wolf, but the wolf soon realized this. Using agility and speed he began shifting back and forth, trying to attack the pig from the side. Within moments Peter was bleeding from three slashes around his shoulders. While not deep they bled quickly, leaving the angry pig looking awful.

The wolf wasn't getting off easy, though. Peter made him pay for every one of the slashes with a bite in return and soon the blood was flowing steadily from his wounds too.

"What's the matter, wolfie?" laughed Peter. "Thought I was a pushover, did you? What do you think now?"

"I think you can't keep this up, fatso. I'm going to keep running circles around you until you drop," snarled the wolf in response. The wolf smiled as he saw the brief hint of acknowledgement in the eyes of Peter that he was right. The pig was already wheezing hard and an occasional ragged breath was loud enough to be heard by all.

Peter needn't have worried. Without warning a large rock sailed out of nowhere and smashed into the back of the wolf's head, knocking him out cold. Looking around for the source Peter heard a wild, chattering laugh from above. Standing on the edge of the roof of the old human's trailer was Buster the monkey and his wife Betty, who had carried a couple of rocks up with them. Both were jumping up and down, giddy with success over Buster's throw of the rock.

"Thank you!" wheezed the pig as the two monkeys waved acknowledgement and a group of rabbits began tying up the unconscious wolf. Turning to other foes the monkeys began picking big clumps of moss from the roof and began flinging these into the eyes of every predator close enough to hit. One of the crows saw what was happening and dodging the shot aimed at him, came hard straight at Buster.

Buster screeched laughter in response. Just as it seemed the crow was about to claw and peck him badly the monkey made a quick, nimble move to the side and leapt onto the back of the surprised bird. The two animals rolled back and forth on the roof as the crow struggled to get free from the clawing, biting monkey. The fight took them too close to the edge, however, and with a despairing squawk of fear from the bird they both tumbled off the roof.

With an audible crunching sound they landed hard on the old human's back porch. Unfortunately for the crow, he was on the bottom when they landed and was knocked unconscious. A group of stick bugs quickly descended on him and soon had him all tied up and unable to move even a claw.

The other crow was still flying low chasing after the rabbit children, but suddenly realized he was the focus of a very angry group of desperate animals trying to stop him at any cost. He turned to retreat just in time to take a hard hit to the head from a piece of metal pipe the new stick bug Twiggs wielded. The stunned crow wobbled in flight, trying to regain his senses. With the first crow out of the fight, however, all of the slingshot groups could now focus on the remaining bird. A massive barrage of rocks dropped him from the air and he was soon stretched out unconscious, firmly tied up beside the first crow.

The remaining wolves had been doing better than the crows, but the tide had turned. One had finally been surrounded by a crowd of animals wielding sharpened spears and wasn't going anywhere. Several distracted him with a determined frontal assault while a group behind him managed to set a rope trap and catch his hind legs. In no time he was as firmly tied up as the two crows and the first wolf. The remaining two wolves, however, were still creating havoc. Four animals had been clawed or bitten badly and more were being threatened.

The engineer rabbits brought out another surprise to exact their revenge on the remaining two wolves. "Lets go, gang, they need us out there!" urged Twitch. A little group of rabbits came into view pulling a makeshift cart with wheels. On top of the cart was a huge slingshot. Stopping it some distance from the fight they anchored the cart in place by putting blocks on the wheels.

The clever rabbits had built their big slingshot well. The platform it sat on was stable enough to support the handle of the slingshot, which sat in a strong, hollow metal tube bolted to the platform. The force of the sling being pulled back was fully supported and best of all it gave a wide range of motion. As targets moved the slingshot could be rotated to aim properly to ensure the target was hit.

Twitch wasted no time once it was set up. "Lets go boys, a nice big rock for that wolf on the left. Ready? Fire!!!"

Their aim was perfect, striking the unsuspecting wolf on the side of the head and dropping him flat. The one remaining wolf, seeing what had happened, looked around for help. Finding only enemies, he did the only thing he could do. Lunging with speed and desperation, he went after the nearest animal he could find to take a hostage. This was Oscar the cat, who with equally desperate speed just escaped the clutches of the wolf. Unfortunately for Windy, the wolf's lunging miss meant he was now closest to her. Without time to take her eyes off the wolf she kept leaping desperately backwards as he tried to trap her with his paws.

With a scream Twiggs the stick bug attacked the wolf, pounding him hard on the side of his head. The distraction was just enough to divert the wolf from certain capture of Windy at the last second. And by then, it was far too late.

"Fire!!!" screamed Sticks. A virtual avalanche of rocks was launched from all directions at the wolf. Completely stunned, he could offer no resistance as the Junk Town animals surrounded him with a forest of sharp spears. In short order he and the other wolves were lying on the ground beside each other, all tied up and unable to move, just like the crows.

The defenders were exhausted, but jubilant. Several Junk Town animals went to Peter the pig and Buster the monkey to thank them for their help.

"Well, that was exciting!" chittered the monkey. "Does that happen often around here?"

"I sure hope not," said the pig. "I'm going to have to exercise and lose some weight if it does. That wolf was right, he would have run circles around me."

Windy, meanwhile, had recovered from the fright of being stalked by the wolf. Running over to where Twiggs was leaning on his stick she gave him a big hug. "My hero! Thank you Twiggs, you saved me again!"

Twiggs just grinned and hugged her back. "I like saving pretty girls, especially ones that want to give me a hug."

Sticks had come over to check on her and saw the whole interaction between them. He turned to leave, but Windy stopped him. "Did you want us, Sticks?"

"Ah, I was just wanting to check on you to make sure you were okay. That wolf almost had you, but it looks like you're in good hands here so I'll move on. We've got a few others that didn't come through this so well."

There were several others in need of help. The border rat that had stood his ground to help the refugees fleeing to Junk Town for safety was in very bad shape. A number of rats stood clustered around him. Several other animals had been slashed or had other small wounds and bruises.

Sticks came up to join the group around the rat just as one of the female rats in the group wailed in despair and began to cry. Several others hugged her, shaking their heads. Sticks saw Sniff the rat leader standing clenching his fists and staring into the distance.

"Sniff?" asked Sticks in a tentative voice. "What's happening?"

Sniff turned and Sticks could see the anger and anguish playing on the rats face. For a long moment he said nothing, but then he heaved a ragged sigh. "He's gone, Sticks."

Sticks groaned and placed his hand on the rats shoulder to comfort him. "Ah, I'm sorry to hear this. We're going to have to do better next time."

"He was my nephew, Sticks, a good kid. He stood his ground and took on that wolf. He saved all those other poor rats trying to get to safety here." A grim look of anger built on the rats face as he gripped the stick in his hands and turned, looking over to where the captive predators lay on the ground. "I'm going to beat that wolf to a pulp."

"Hang on, Sniff," said Sticks, giving him a gentle touch on the shoulder. The rat paused, looking hard at Sticks.

"I know you want to make them pay for this. But you can't just go and beat a helpless prisoner to death. We're better than that, remember?" The rat just kept glaring at Sticks as he continued. "They're predators, Sniff. They're just doing what predators are meant to do, trying to find food and stay alive. We don't have to like it. And we're just defending ourselves. If we'd managed to kill one of them while defending ourselves they probably wouldn't like it either."

"Gah!" snorted the rat, his anger still evident. Sniff abruptly stalked away to stand by himself and stare into the distance. Knowing the rat needed time to himself, Sticks went over to the rest of the rats still clustered about the grieving mother. After spending a few minutes with them he was just leaving as Sniff came back to talk to him once again.

"Yeah, all right, I get it." The rat rubbed his face and shook his head in frustration. "Good thing you're the Mayor around here, you keep a cooler head than anyone I know, including me. But what are we going to do with this bunch? Sticks, we need to make them pay for this, somehow. If we turn them loose they're just going to regroup and come back again. We've got to do something!" pleaded the rat.

"Ah," replied Sticks, giving Sniff a tiny smile of encouragement. "I completely agree. Hey, I'd personally enjoy turning Stuff loose on this bunch, but I think we can do better than that. And here comes my friend Twitch, who I think wants to talk about this too."

"Well, we have some captives, Sticks," said the rabbit, a grim smile on his face. "Think its time we gave it a try?"

"Oh, yes. Absolutely. Scar and Spike have forgotten that it's a real bad idea to mess with us. Time for a reminder." Sticks turned to Sniff and put a gentle hand on his shoulder once again. "We can't bring your nephew back, but I think you're going to like this. We have some very clever rabbits around here!"

Chapter Four

The frustrated snarls of the wolves and angry squawks from the crows at the indignity of it all was music to ears of the Junk Town animals. Several children were rolling on the ground laughing while others danced back and forth in front of the humbled predators.

The group of six engineer rabbits working on the captives grinned as the final touches were added by one of their number. He stepped back and to the side, gesturing at the wolves and crows as the others joined him. "Well, everyone, what do you think?"

The watching crowd roared and applauded in response and the engineer rabbits took a collective bow. Rawk stepped forward and smiled at the rabbits. "You guys are hired for my next show!"

"So what do you think, Sniff?" said Sticks, moving to stand next to the rat. "Does this work for you?"

"Yeah," replied the rat, a bleak smile on his face. "Yes, it does. The family is happy with this, too."

"Good. Okay, that means its time to get this ugly crowd out of our sight." Turning, he signaled to a waiting group of animals armed with spears and slingshots. Seeing his signal they immediately stiffened in readiness.

Not that it was likely they would be needed. Sticks stepped forward and glared at the angry captives, who grew silent realizing they were about to learn their fate.

"Right. So I hope all of you realize you are at our mercy. We could take you and dump you in the creek right now and watch you slowly sink into oblivion. Lots of animals around here have even better ideas than that." Sticks paused a moment to let that sink in, then continued. "However, we're choosing to use you to send a message instead. It's so simple even you idiots can get it. And the message is you're going to pay if you mess with us!"

Sticks took a long moment to glare hard at each one of the still silent predators. "Now get lost and take that message back to your leaders."

Looking around, he nodded at the waiting rabbit engineers. Coming forward they began using the sharp edge of their spears to cut the bonds that held the trapped predators. A loud tinkling sound was heard as the first was freed and soon the sound was everywhere in the air, along with more snorts of laughter from the Junk Town animals.

Although the predators were now free of the tight bonds holding them they were still not entirely free. The rabbits had tied a sack with a heavy, large rock in it to each of their legs. Each of them had a similar sack and rock around their neck, all of which effectively limited their ability to move to a very slow walk.

That wasn't all, however. The tinkling sound came from a tight leather collar with bells on it that had also been fastened around the necks of each animal. Even the slightest of movements set the bells to tinkling loudly.

Rawk couldn't resist teasing the predators. "Hey, guys, you could be the rhythm section in my

next show if you coordinate your moves! No?
Well, if nothing else I could use you all as clowns!"

"Well, I guess we should tell the truth,
Rawk," said Twitch. "The idea for this started from
one of your shows with the clowns. You like the
color scheme?"

Rawk nodded and laughed. "Oh yes.
They're so bright they'll be seen from miles away."

The final indignity had been to paint the
predators with an insane rainbow of bright colors.
The humbled predators could only glare in
humiliation as they turned to shuffle away, prodded
by the sharp spears of the Junk Town animals. A
couple of the wolves tried hard to lift their paws to
swat at their captors. They quickly realized the
rocks made any such move impossible and, worse,
just earned them several jabs from the sharp spears
of the Junk Town animals. One of the crows tried
his best to fly off, but immediately fell flat on his
face because the weight of the rocks made that
impossible too.

The merry, tinkling sound of the captives
shuffling away dwindled and was soon gone. Sniff
finally turned from watching them leave and looked
at Sticks and Twitch. "It's times like this I wish I
was a bird and could fly. I'd love to be hiding in
the trees watching that crowd having to report to
their bosses. The best part would be the look on
Scar and Spike's faces!"
                        ***

The crowd around the fire that night had
mixed emotions. On the one hand several animals
had been hurt and one lost. However, the success
of their defense and the thorough humiliation of

the predators was cause for optimism. More than a
few animals had privately feared their successful
defense in the Battle of Junk Town last Fall had
been a lucky fluke. Although this time there had
been only a half dozen predators involved in the
attack, their defeat was complete and hopefully
enough to make the others think twice before
trying it again.

The newcomers to Junk Town were all very
optimistic for the future and all were vocal about it.
Peter the pig was overjoyed that his new 'herd' had
crushed the attackers so thoroughly. "Come on,
guys, this is great! We need to celebrate a victory.
Anyone want to dance?"

Rawk just smiled as he watched the pig
dance around the fire by himself. "Hmm, I think
you could have a bright future. Not real graceful,
but you make up for it with enthusiasm! I'll work
you into a spot for the next show."

The mood lightened as the evening wore
on. In the midst of it Windy, Twiggs, and a couple
of the other new stick bugs approached Sticks and
Twitch, curious looks on their faces.

"Hi guys," she said, giving Sticks a broad
smile. "We just wanted to say thanks for
everything. It's been such a relief to settle in here.
We feel safe now!"

"Well, it's a group effort to make it that
way," replied Sticks. "But it looks to me like you've
got more on your mind than this?"

"Ah, yes, we were curious about the
'message' you sent today. We know you suggested
the predators could easily have been dumped in the

stream and left to drown. I guess we're curious, would you actually have done that?"

Sticks and Twitch looked hard at each other, then back at Windy before Sticks finally responded. "Hmm, well, no, not likely. We certainly could have done that, but the question is really why we would do that? I suppose if any of us wanted them as food it might be different, but we don't. And killing them just because they're chasing us for their own food doesn't serve any purpose, does it?"

Windy and the other stick bugs all looked at each other, then looked back at Sticks and Twitch. "How about all the things you did to them, out of curiosity? It's going to be very hard for those wolves and crows to feed themselves in future."

This time Twitch smiled and replied. "Yes, but they won't starve. The thing is, they'll be able to get those rocks we tied around their feet off in short order. They just have to rub the ropes against something sharp and they'll come off. The paint will all wash off sooner or later too. Now, the bells, those will be another matter!"

"How come?" said one of the other stick bugs with a deep, curious look on his face.

Twitch laughed. "You'd be amazed what you can find in a junk yard and how creative my engineers are. We worked long and hard to make those collars with the bells real sturdy and durable. They're made of very strong, tough leather and we attached them nice and tight with a strong clasp that needs a little key to open it. They won't be able to just slip them over their head and it'll take a long time to wear through the leather."

"But what will they eat if they can't catch anything?" asked Windy.

Twitch just shrugged. "That's their problem. Hey, if our friend Stuff the bear can get along just fine eating berries and raiding bee's nests for honey, I'm sure they can too. They can scavenge for dead salmon after they spawn. Lots of choices, right? The main thing is we'll hear them coming a mile away as long as they have those bells on."

The newcomers all turned and looked at each other, incredulous looks on their faces. Windy finally turned back to Sticks and Twitch and as she did a tear slipped from the corner of one eye. Twiggs placed a supportive hand on her shoulder and Windy gave it a grateful momentary squeeze.

Sticks was stunned. "Say, are you okay?"

"Yes, sure, I'm fine," said Windy, a little smile growing on her face as she wiped the tear from her eye. "Sorry, you're probably wondering what this is all about. It's just we're so grateful Rawk invited us here. We had a really hard time before coming here, you see. There were eighteen of us when we were first abandoned. The predators got them, of course."

Sticks and Twitch looked at each other. "Well, we owe a big debt to Rawk, too," replied Sticks. "We'd likely have been food for someone too were it not for him."

"But that's not all, Sticks. It's just, well, we've been very surprised at your approach to the predators." A puzzled look appeared on his face as she continued hastily. "Sorry, that's surprised in a good way! See, life in the forest has just seemed so, so..."

"Harsh," said one of the other stick bugs.

"Brutal," said Twiggs.

"Yes. It's been a fight to the death every day for us. And if we could have killed any of the predators that got our people we would have done so. But you guys, well, you just boot them out of town after thoroughly humiliating them! So I guess I'm just trying to say we like the change in approach."

"Sure," replied Twitch, smiling at Sticks. "Well, it's mostly our fearless leader here that brought that about. Seriously, though, everyone here saw the logic. You have to ask yourself what point there would be with a harsher approach."

"Yeah," said Sticks. "If something isn't going to be my dinner I see no reason for being 'harsh'. All life is important, don't you think? Who are we to make life and death decisions over someone else, unless you're in the middle of a no holds barred fight? I just think we've got choice."

A silence descended as an odd look stole over Windy's face once again. Sticks and Twitch were about to speak when she stepped forward and gave Twitch a hug. "We don't know how to thank you! Thank you both from all of us!"

Turning, she gave Sticks a hug and planted a quick kiss on the surprised stick bugs cheek. "You have no idea how grateful we are. This seems like heaven to us and I think you two are responsible for it being that way." Stepping back, she smiled sheepishly. "Your dinner's are getting cold. I'll leave you be." Windy turned a final time, with a quick glance back at Sticks and they all returned to their table.

Leaf had meanwhile been sitting to the side watching the entire exchange. Slipping over to stand beside Sticks and Twitch as she watched the others walk away she whispered to Sticks from the side of her mouth. "Hey, bro, I think you've got a fan there."

"Uh," replied Sticks. "Yes, they seem grateful to be here. Nice to know we're appreciated, right, Twitch?"

"No, I don't think that's what your dear sister is talking about, Sticks. She means you have a fan there."

"Eh? What do you mean?"

Turning, Twitch gave Sticks a curious look. "I trust you noticed that all I got was a hug. You got a hug and a kiss. Not that I'm jealous, you understand. Hmm, well, maybe I am, come to think of it. She's pretty!"

"Oh," said Sticks, blushing a little. "Huh. I think you're both reading things that aren't there into this. Lets go eat."

Chapter Five

The Junk Town animals were all wary over
the next few days. No one knew how the predators
would react to such a stunning humiliation of some
of their number. Privately, several animals were
expecting it would drive Scar and his pack berserk
and bring a massive attack in retaliation. They were
surprised when the next intruder crossing the
border of Junk Town was not a pack of angry
predators.

This time it was the monkey family,
swinging about high in the trees, giving the
warning. "Everyone!" screeched Buster. "A car
just drove up and stopped at the gate. I think
there's a human trying to get into the junk yard!"

The Junk Town animals all stopped what
they were doing in stunned surprise. They'd seen
no humans at all in Junk Town since last fall when
the police officers had searched the old human's
trailer and locked everything up. It brought back
unpleasant memories of a devastating day, learning
their protector had passed away in town. In a
collective rush they all ran to find out what was
happening.

The Junk Town animals were a well-trained
group, however. They knew their standing orders
should something like this occur were to stay quiet
and hidden until more was known.

What they found was a lone, middle aged
human female fumbling with a ring of keys, trying
each in turn on the lock that held the rusty chain
across the entrance to Junk Town. "Ah, finally,"
she muttered as the lock snapped open. Throwing

the chain to the side she went to her car and drove it in, stopping in front of the old trailer.

She got out of the car once again, but to everyone's surprise she just stood looking around for several long moments. Visibly steeling herself, she walked over to the trailer and fumbled with the chain of keys once again. Finding the right one she opened the door and groaned aloud to herself as she looked inside. "Dad! Oh, it's even worse than I thought it would be. How am I ever going to deal with this?"

She disappeared, stepping inside, but not for long. Less than five minutes later she came back out, groaning and brushing dust and cobwebs off her clothes. Instead of returning to her car she walked off to explore the piles of junk that stretched into the distance. Returning ten minutes later she rounded the corner of the trailer and saw the homes of the Junk Town animals laid out between the trailer and the old barn over by the fence. Skidding to a full stop, her jaw dropped open.

The animals waited silently in hiding, wondering what she would do. The woman finally stepped forward and looked closer at some of the dwellings. Shaking her head, she stood back and softly groaned once again.

"Wow. I have no idea what he was doing here. And I don't want to know." With a final glance, she turned away and went back into the trailer.

Emerging an hour later she made sure the trailer was once again locked and she drove her car back out to the road. Locking the chain across the entrance she gave one final look around and drove away.

The Junk Town animals slowly emerged from hiding and converged together around Sticks in the clearing in front of the trailer.

"Well, what do you make of that, Sticks?" asked Harry the tarantula.

Sticks stood staring after the departing car for a moment, then gave a weary shake of his head. "I don't know. I seem to remember the old human said he had a daughter somewhere. Perhaps she just paid us a visit. I think she said 'Dad', didn't she? Aside from that I have no idea. Anybody have thoughts here?"

"I think you're right, Sticks," replied Twitch slowly. "But beyond that I have no idea. Mystery woman didn't leave us many clues to work with."

No one else had anything to offer either. Just before they broke up, however, one of the engineer rabbits tugged at Twitch's arm. "Hey, Twitch? We've got company again. Over there, about three big branches down, second tree from the fence."

There was no stopping the animals that heard him from looking. Sure enough, a large crow was watching while trying to hide from view. Seeing he was discovered, he hopped into plain view and glared at the animals below. With an angry squawk he took to the air, catching them off guard as he swooped in a low arc over the heads of the surprised crowd. Squawking laughter, the crow flew off.

"Yeah, you'd better run!" screamed Sniff the rat shaking a fist after him. "You won't get away with that a second time!"

"Right, well, now everyone knows what happened here today," said Sticks.

"You think this is going to be a problem, Sticks?" asked one of the dogs.

"I don't know. Honestly. I guess we have to assume that was the old human's daughter, but what she's going to do we'll have to wait and see. As for the crow, well, I guess we shouldn't be surprised they're being persistent, should we?"

***

The days passed and turned into weeks. The woman didn't return and the predators made no serious attempts to attack Junk Town. Crows were seen hiding in the trees, watching almost all the time. Even wolves were seen, hiding the in the low bushes around the trees. Initially, neither the crows nor the wolves made any effort to attack.

After a few weeks the probes of their defenses resumed. The Junk Town defenders couldn't help but be amused, however. Several of the predators testing their defenses turned out to be the same group of wolves and crows that they'd defeated earlier in the Spring.

As Twitch predicted they had managed to get the rocks off their legs and from around their necks. The paint had almost worn off too, and wasn't as bright as when it had first been put on, but faded patches were still evident. The wolves just scowled and slunk away to the laughter of the Junk Town defenders whenever they were seen.

Twitch was also right about the bell collars, all still firmly in place around their necks. The predators tried to muffle the sound every time they approached, but could be successful for only a few moments. On each occasion it was soon very clear to the Junk Town defenders enemies were coming.

Instead of rushing to the attack these were a series of careful, slow probes trying to find and identify the traps the engineer rabbits had set. Walking up in a slow, random approach to a new and different spot on the defensive perimeter they carefully scanned the environment at each point they approached. The Junk Town defenders soon realized what they were doing and the game evolved into a race to see whether the predators could learn where the traps were before being driven off with a hail of rocks.

Sticks and Twitch had regular conversations over what was happening as they came to understand what the predators were doing. "Persistent, aren't they?" said Twitch. "But why do you think it's this same crowd of fools we sent packing in the Spring?"

"Good question," replied Sticks, a puzzled look on his face. "You'd think they'd have better success by using recruits that aren't wearing bells."

"Yeah. Okay, why don't we ask them?"

Sticks just smiled. "Sure. Could be amusing if nothing else."

Both were ready for it when the next probe came two days later. The Junk Town border defenders had been instructed to let the wolves get a little closer than usual and then hold fire until Sticks and Twitch could get there.

They found a pair of male, belled wolves caught in the act of trying to probe near the edges of a trap they'd found and glaring at the defenders as they did. A puzzled look was in their eyes too, trying to understand why they weren't being pelted with rocks as had happened every other time they'd approached.

Sticks and Twitch stepped forward and the wolves stopped, recognizing both animals from their previous encounter. The puzzled looks disappeared and were replaced with looks burning with anger.

"Hello ugly ones," said Sticks. "How's life in the forest?"

Both wolves gave an angry snort in response and glared in harsh anger at the stick bug. Seeing Sticks was serious about a conversation, they looked at each other and then back at the stick bug. "Why do you care?" growled one of them.

"Just curious. You all seem rather persistent about coming back here, although I'd have thought this was the last place any of you would want to see again."

"Not our idea to be here," snorted the younger of the two wolves. "This is thanks to you."

"If it was up to me the only reason I'd be back here would be to rip all of you to shreds and have a feast!" snarled the older, male wolf. "And sooner or later we will be back to do exactly that!"

"Ah, I get it!" said Sticks. "This is punishment, isn't it?" The wolves just glared back, murderous looks on their faces confirming he was right, so Sticks continued. "Yeah, you guys didn't get the expected result when you attacked us, did you? We embarrassed you and your boss badly, so Scar is making you probe our defenses. You get to be the ones getting shot at with rocks every time you come here. Must be nice to have a boss that cares so much about you! Really, why don't you just leave all that? Go somewhere else a long ways away, start your own wolf pack?"

The older wolf snorted in response and shook his head. "Shows what you know about wolves. Once you're in the pack, you're in. There is no getting out."

"Really? No one's ever tried to leave?"

The two wolves looked at each other once again, before turning back to Sticks. "Yeah, there have been a few. But they have to go a long, long ways away and be very, very good to survive. The pack makes a point of hunting them down and the pack is real good at hunting. They're either cowards who can't take it anymore or they try to become competition, see?"

"Wow. Sounds like a pretty harsh life either way. So what about another option? Would you consider something else?"

Both wolves narrowed their eyes in puzzlement. "Another option? What are you talking about?"

"Join us."

Several of the Junk Town defenders jaws dropped and every animal present looked at Sticks in stunned silence. Sticks just looked mildly back at the shocked wolves, finally deciding to break the silence. "I'm serious, you know."

"That's ridiculous!" snorted the older wolf. "I mean, wake up here, you're our prey. You're my future dinner. I don't know what you're talking about."

"Well, I do," replied Sticks. "I'm telling you it doesn't have to be this way. You don't have to be part of Scar's pack. You can join us. We have lots of fun together, probably way more than you'd ever have hanging around with Scar. Of course, you'll have to play by our rules."

"Rules?"

"Sure. Rule number one is you can't try and eat anyone living in Junk Town. You know, just be nice to everyone. Rule number two is you have to help defend us if we're attacked. Everyone here agrees to these rules and that's pretty much it." Sticks paused, as a sheepish look came over his face. "Well, there is another rule about having to wear a chicken hat if you're grouchy and make everyone unhappy."

The wolves looked at each other once again, still bewildered. "But we need prey to eat. I don't see how that could work," said the younger wolf.

"Look, you're not the only predators around here. The cats eat the mice they catch. Harry the tarantula eats crickets. The dogs are getting real partial to eating fish from the stream. They actually caught a small deer a while back, too. And Stuff the bear? Well, need I say more?"

The wolves just stared back in stunned silence. The older wolf finally shook his head hard, as if he was trying to clear his mind. "This is nonsense!" he growled, looking hard at the younger wolf. "It's a trick! He's just trying to lure us into some trap. Let's get out of here!"

"Are you sure?" said the younger wolf, a strange look on his face.

"Are you crazy? You fool! Even if he isn't lying through his teeth you know Scar would go mad if we were to do anything like that. And I don't even want to think about the consequences. Besides, he is trying to trick us. Come on!"

Turning, both wolves slunk away, heading into the underbrush. The younger wolf was the last to go and he paused for the briefest of moments to look back at Sticks, the odd look still on his face. Then he was gone.

Sticks remained standing and watching for several long moments before finally turning to leave. He stopped short, looking around to see none of the Junk Town defenders had moved from where they stood. They were all staring hard at him with strange, unreadable looks on their faces. Sticks looked slowly back and forth at the waiting crowd before finally breaking the silence.

"What? Come on gang, out with it."

Shadow the cat finally spoke up. "Uh, Sticks, were you really serious about that invitation?"

"Sure. Well, to be honest, I wasn't real optimistic about them taking me up on it."

"Yeah," said one of the border guard rats. "But if you make an invitation you have to be prepared they might actually do it."

"Of course. Okay, look, you all think I'm crazy, right?" Seeing a few of the animals wearing sheepish looks, he continued. "I saw an opportunity to grow a little more discontent among their ranks. You saw the look on that young wolf's face? He was tempted. And I'm hoping he'll go back and talk to some of the others."

"You're right, Sticks, I saw that too. I thought that young wolf might actually accept the offer for a brief second there," said Twitch.

"Yeah. Who knows, maybe he'll show up on our doorstep wanting in some day?"

"So you think that could actually work, Sticks?" replied Twitch, a curious look on his face.

Sticks paused a long moment, composing his thoughts. "Well, yes. Yes, I do. Look, I admit this was a spur of the moment thing, but I do think it could work. And I do think it very possible we could get a new recruit. Think about being a member of a pack of predators where life every day was just downright harsh and miserable. Now think about having an opportunity to live in a place where life may still be hard, but its not unpleasant and can even be fun sometimes. Well, sounds tempting, right?"

"You don't think the temptation to suddenly turn and eat one of us would be too great?"

"Who knows? But if we make sure any new wolf recruit is fed and happy, why would he? I don't know, I guess I believe everyone is capable of changing, even wolves." Sticks paused again for a moment to compose his next words. "See, you can call me crazy, but I figure wolves are just as important in this world as we are. I also think a little kindness will always work wonders. Besides, maybe Rawk could use a real wolf in his shows?"

Several animals chuckled at that. As it died down and silence slowly returned, Sticks looked around at the watching group once again. Then one of the rabbits began to slowly clap his hands. Several others joined in and within moments they were all applauding the stick bug.

Twitch spoke up as it began to die off. "Looks like everyone agrees with you, Sticks. I knew there was a reason we made you the Mayor of this place!"

Lyle Garford

Chapter Six

The probes of their defenses continued.
Over time more of the wolves that hadn't been
belled started to be involved, but as before no
effort was being made to actually attack. The
watching crows were a constant presence in the
trees, trying to stay hidden. Sometimes the two
crows with bells made sudden, bold swoops over
the Junk Town animals working in their gardens. A
hail of rocks forced them to leave fast every time.

The constant probes made Sticks and
Twitch both feel Scar and Spike were plotting
something big once again. That meant regularly
drilling the Junk Town animals in defense and
urging them to be wary.

The problem was they didn't want to be
wary. The weather had been steadily improving,
bringing smiles to everyone along with the warmer
days. Spring was almost over and summer was fast
approaching. With it was the date for the big
wedding of Wally and Leaf. They both wanted
everything to be perfect and waiting till the start of
summer in order to get the best possible weather
made sense.

Wally grew more nervous and distracted
every day. Leaf and the Mom stick bug, busy
organizing the wedding, were soon completely fed
up with him. "Sticks," pleaded Leaf. "Can't you do
something with him? He's completely useless to us
and is walking around in a fog. Mom alternates
between wanting to throttle him and telling me we
should just elope!""

63

Sticks just smiled. "Hmm. I think that could be easily solved. Leave it to me."

That night around the fire after dinner Sticks and Twitch were deep in conversation before finally calling Wally over to join them. Pitching his voice loud enough to ensure everyone heard the call made them all turn their attention in their direction, knowing Sticks never did anything like that without a reason.

Wally knew it too. "Hello mates. What's up? You two have something in the works."

"Well, yes, actually. We were thinking everyone needs a break around here. We've been pushing everyone pretty hard to stay well drilled for our defenses on top of taking care of all our regular chores. I figure we'll have a mutiny if we try doing one more drill," said Sticks.

"Glad you figured that out before we actually did it," nodded Wally.

"Right. Anyway, we noticed that pretty much the entire forest has been invited to your wedding. We were thinking maybe we should get them to come a little early. Specifically, we thought we could talk you into organizing a pre-wedding soccer tournament? They're all going to be here anyway, right?"

Wally's eyes immediately lit up as he began to consider the possibilities, so Sticks continued. "Thing is, there are going to be way too many animals wanting to play, right?"

Wally nodded as several of the animals listening in the background began cheering support for the idea. Holding up a hand to hold off further interruptions Twitch spoke up for the first time.

"As much fun as it is to just have the Junk Town All Stars take on the Squirrel Soccer Nuts, why don't you do it differently this time? You've got enough good players you could put together at least seven or eight teams. Do a round robin tournament, you know, each team plays the other then you have a playoff."

"Brilliant, mates!" said Wally. Then he paused and looked over at where Leaf and Mom stick bug were sitting. "Uh, but if we take everyone away to practice is this going to be a problem for wedding preparations?"

The women just smiled. "Just go do it, sweetheart. Please!" said Leaf.

"Right, well, I don't think there's anyone better than you to organize this, Wally. It's all yours," said Sticks.

The listening crowd roared, all trying to get Wally's attention at the same time. An eager group of animals was soon clustered around Wally discussing how it could work. After several minutes of animated conversation it came to sudden halt and, almost as one, the group turned and looked at Twitch.

"Uh, Twitch, small problem. We have only one soccer field," said Wally, a sheepish look on his face.

Twitch laughed. "I was wondering how long it would take you guys to figure that out. Not to worry, we've already got a plan to build another. There's a spot on the far side of the stage by the fence that'll serve. We won't be able to have as many seats around it, but it'll do. Let us know if that will be enough. If it isn't I'm pretty sure we can build a third one for you."

The crowd standing around Wally all smiled in relief and went back to their plans with delight.

***

What they hadn't counted on was Rawk's ambition on top of this. He'd deliberately not done a show for the animals for several weeks, knowing he was in charge of the entertainment for the wedding night and wanting to save his best for it. Several animals suddenly found themselves with a number of routines to learn and practice.

With Sticks still wanting the animals to practice defensive drills, Leaf needing things done for the wedding, Rawk demanding more practice for routines, and Wally trying to organize teams for soccer the result was a crazed, uncoordinated frenzy of activity. Several animals found themselves expected to be in two places at the same time on several occasions.

The newcomers to Junk Town were amazed. "This is like a giant anthill being invaded by an army of anteaters," said Buster to his wife as they dodged to avoid being trampled by a large group of rabbit engineers bustling past.

Somehow, it all got done. Word of the tournament spread far and wide via the forest animals. Rawk seemed tireless. When he wasn't reviewing the progress of the animals learning their routines he flew off in all different directions to spread the word. Coming back from an extended trip he brought with him the same eagle family that had helped win the Battle of Junk Town last Fall.

Now that the weather was warmer they'd returned to their favorite spots to hunt.

"Look who I found!" said Rawk, landing near Sticks and Twitch with the majestic eagles in tow. "They were hanging out around that other place I came across in the spring. They've got some animals there too! I must learn more about it when I have more time. Say, Twitch, I hope you're ready for this. I think this place is going to be packed!"

They were indeed ready. The rabbit engineers had built several temporary shelters on one edge of town for the sudden influx of forest animals now steadily arriving. Several of Twitch's wild rabbit cousins took up residence, as did a small army of forest squirrels.

A few animals they'd never seen before appeared too. The unexpected group of skunks that arrived got an immediate, wary reaction, but they politely assured everyone they had heard about it all and wanted to join the fun. After assurances no one would be sprayed room was found for them on the edge of town. A large family of quail with perfect camouflage coloring appeared one day too, startling the border guard with their sudden appearance. A host of other forest birds filled the air, flying from perch to perch.

The soccer tournament required a full two days to play out, meaning the only opportunity to practice for the wedding party was the day before the tournament started. However, Sticks had yet another dilemma to work around when Wally asked him to be his best man just as they were getting organized for the rehearsal.

"Sure!" said Sticks. "I'm honored, Wally. But aren't you forgetting something?"

Wally looked puzzled. "What?"

"Well, I am the mayor after all." Seeing Wally still didn't get it, he continued. "Remember? I'm supposed to be conducting the actual marriage ceremony for you. I can't be in two places at once."

"Ah. Right," said Wally, looking crestfallen. "Well, you've been my best friend since you came here. I couldn't think of anyone better."

"Hmm," replied Sticks. "Okay, if that's what you want, why don't I get Twitch to be deputy Mayor and have him do the ceremony?" Wally smiled in agreement so Sticks went to talk to Twitch.

For her bridesmaid Leaf had chosen Windy. The two young females had become fast friends since Windy had come to Junk Town and she readily accepted the role.

They all gathered around Mom stick bug the day before the soccer tournament so she could explain what had been planned in order to do the rehearsal. Sticks joined the others gathered leaning over the table Mom was seated at using a diagram to explain it all.

Sticks wasn't watching where he placed his hand as he looked to support himself while leaning forward to see the diagram. Windy was standing beside him, one hand holding the top of a chair for her own support. When his hand came down on hers the sensation of touching her soft hand was electric.

"Oh!" said Windy. Both turned, unnoticed by the others, to look at his hand on top of hers. As they both looked up stunned, neither made any effort to remove their hands for a long moment as they both stared into each other's eyes.

"Ah, sorry," mumbled Sticks in sudden haste, finally removing his hand. "I wasn't watching what I was doing."

Windy gave him a searching look and reached up to briefly touch his shoulder. "It's okay. We should get back to this."

"Right," said Sticks, turning his attention back to the conversation still going on in front of them. As he did, he felt Twiggs staring at him, standing on the other side of the table listening in. The look on his face was unreadable. Offering a hesitant smile, the only thing Sticks could do was turn to focus his attention back on the conversation. Sticks felt like he was in a fog the rest of the rehearsal, but somehow managed to get through it without further embarrassment.

***

By the time the soccer tournament was ready to start the number of new animals wandering around Junk Town was overwhelming.

Sticks stopped by to see Twitch, who seemed frenetic as he issued orders to a steady stream of animals looking for answers. "Are you okay?" asked Sticks.

"Uh, yeah, hang on a second," replied Twitch, a sudden stressed look on his face as a group of engineer rabbits needing more orders clarified appeared. Twitch came back, looking in all directions before stopping in front of Sticks.

"Wow, Mr. Mayor. I knew this was going to get busy, but this is almost crazy. We've got it more or less under control, though, I think."

"Yeah, I think the only animals left in the forest are the wolves and the crows. And I rather think they're watching all this with interest from a distance. Who knows? Maybe they're even jealous!"

Neither was concerned, though. The sheer numbers of animals present gave them the confidence they could fight off even the most substantial and determined attack.

The lumbering presence of Stuff the bear helped too. Even better, he didn't arrive alone. Everyone was soon introduced to Honey, the young female bear he had in tow. The Junk Town animals all applauded the proud pair as they announced they were engaged and would eventually be married too.

The soccer tournament was a wild success. Wally had finally limited the number of teams to eight. The Squirrel Soccer Nuts had split into two teams, the Acorns and the Peanuts, while the Junk Town All Stars had turned into four more teams. The monkey family recruited a mixed group of newcomers to Junk Town along with some from the All Stars, and now led a team called Monkey Business. Twitch's jackrabbit cousin from the forest had organized a team called The Rabbit Runners from the ranks of his relatives to complete the roster.

Everyone was pleasantly exhausted by the end of the second day of games. Competition had been fierce, but it had finally come down to two teams going for the championship. The squirrels had cleverly stacked the Acorns team with all of their very best players and demolished all of their opponents along the way to the final.

Wally just snorted with laughter when he saw their lineup. "Cheeky bunch, aren't they?" he said to Sticks. "Anyone can see what they're up to."

"No rules about that, Wally," replied Sticks. "You are of course going to counter that, aren't you?"

"Well, I'm not, since I'm running this show and not playing."

Sticks just smiled and raised a questioning eyebrow, as Wally looked sheepish in response.

"Okay, well, I may have offered some advice on player selection to Buster and Betty," he finally confessed, after a furtive look around to ensure no one was listening. "Can't let those rascals have it all their way, now can I?"

The game had the crowd cheering every move throughout. Twiggs the stick bug was a striker with the Monkey Business team. Combining with the monkeys on several plays to dance around the squirrel defenders he scored two hard fought goals. The squirrels were determined to avenge their previous losses in past tournaments, however, and played with incredible speed and precision passes that simply couldn't be matched. The three goals they scored won them the match.

Wally was gracious as he presented the squirrel captain with a trophy the rabbit engineers had built for the occasion. "So, been practicing for this, have we?" said Wally, a broad grin on his face.

The squirrel captain just grinned back. "Ah, maybe just a little." Several members of the crowd snorted with laughter. The unashamed squirrel captain raised the trophy high in the air as their supporters roared and crowded round to celebrate.

Supporters of the Monkey Business team gathered loyally around them too. "You all did well. Those squirrels have obviously had a lot more practice together than you guys," said Windy the stick bug, giving Twiggs a big hug in the process. "And you, Twiggs, what a game! Two goals! I'm proud of you."

Twiggs just grinned and hugged her back. Sticks came over from congratulating the winners to offer the same to the losing team, finding Twiggs still with his arm around Windy's shoulders. "Well done, Twiggs! Being Mayor cuts into my playing time, but some day we'll have to get in a game together."

"Sure!"

Sticks turned to leave as Twiggs began talking to another crowd of supporters that had arrived. Windy stopped him with a hand on his shoulder. "Hey, thank you for organizing all of this. Twiggs was really happy to be able to show what he can do. He's always loved to play soccer. We're so happy here we still can't believe it. Can I fix you a dinner some day to show my appreciation?"

Sticks was surprised. "Uh, well, maybe. Thank you for the offer, but I really don't want to intrude on you and Twiggs. Maybe we can all do a special dinner for everyone and celebrate when this is all over? Anyway, I must run, Twitch wants me for something."

Windy remained staring after him as he left. A curious look crossed her face for a moment before she shrugged and turned back to the crowd still surrounding Twiggs.

Chapter Seven

The first day of summer dawned with a light, golden sunrise that soon turned into the blue skies and warmth Leaf had been hoping for. By mid afternoon when the wedding was due to start it was almost too warm.

The groom was handsome in the black suit coat and hat he'd donned for the occasion. A similar outfit had been provided to Sticks to wear. Both stick bugs scratched their heads, wondering how Leaf and her Mom had managed to put these together or where they found them. With no ready answer, they just shrugged and put them on.

Leaf was positively glowing as she was led through the crowd by a small army of little stick bugs carrying flowers and dribbling petals behind them. She looked stunning, wearing a long white gown that trailed for several feet behind her. Because of the number of animals in Junk Town the only place the wedding could be held was the big soccer field. Even there it was a struggle to fit everyone in and ensure they had a view.

Windy was stunning too, following behind wearing a light cream-colored gown. Sticks realized he was wishing Twiggs wasn't her favorite, acknowledging to himself it wasn't the first time the thought had crossed his mind.

Despite being nervous Wally rose to the occasion, booming out "I do!" for all to hear when the time came. Twitch finished the ceremony and addressed the waiting crowd. "There you go, everyone. Without further ado, I give you Mr. and Mrs. Wally and Leaf stick bug!" As the crowd

roared with deafening approval, Twitch smiled and
looked at Wally. "Well, get on with it. You may
kiss the bride!"

Bending her over backwards just a little
Wally gave her a big kiss as the crowd began
dancing where thcy stood. The crowd didn't want
to stop so Wally and Leaf gave them several deep
bows of thanks.

Rawk finally stepped into the center of the
soccer field and joined Wally and Leaf, motioning
for silence. Getting that took time as the crowd
started laughing the moment he appeared. The
parrot was wearing a pair of large, red plastic
sunglasses on his face and beach flip-flops on his
feet. He also wore a bright yellow shirt with
flowers and surfboards all over it and a string of
flowers around his neck.

"Okay, everyone, the mushy stuff is over
and it's just about time to party! Hey, are you ready
for a beach party? Yeah!"

Strutting and dancing about to music only
he could hear the parrot worked the crowd as only
he could. Finally calling for quiet he addressed the
crowd. "Okay everyone. We need to do a little set
up so go away and relax for a while." Planted
between the two stick bugs with a wing around
each he continued. "First up Wally and Leaf have a
feast like you've never seen ready for you. Then,
well, I just may have a little entertainment for you."

Many in the crowd snorted with laughter as
the parrot grinned back and all three of them began
to dance in unison. "And then Twitch and his
Rabbit RawkStars are going to make you dance

you're feet off for the rest of the night! So go on! Get lost!"

In obedient anticipation the crowd began to disperse. A huge crowd grew around Wally and Leaf waiting to offer their congratulations personally. Meanwhile, a horde of Junk Town animals began setting up tables around them, as Junk Town once again became a hive of activity.

**

"I've never seen so much food," said Sniff the rat in awe.

"Neither have I," muttered Checkers the dog. "We can't possibly eat all this food. It's going to go to waste! This is completely out of control."

"Careful, Checkers!" smiled the rat. "I know you've a job to do as resident grouch around here, but I don't think you want to find yourself wearing a chicken hat all night with this crowd laughing at you!" The dog scowled, but headed for the food anyway as Sniff laughed.

Leaf and her stick bug Mom and their army of helpers had truly outdone themselves. With so many animals to feed the food had been set up buffet style and there appeared to be something for everyone. The spring growing weather had been very good so many fresh vegetables were already available for those wanting them. A mountain of carrots and lettuce awaited the hungry crowd of rabbits. Fresh leaves were in abundance for the stick bugs. Over by the fire a group of cats and dogs were roasting mice as fast as they could. Harry the tarantula was roasting crickets for himself and anyone else that came by wanting to try them.

An enormous bowl of seeds for all the birds took up one entire table.

Even the monkeys had an unexpected treat. They were delighted to find a little bunch of slightly over ripe bananas sitting on the buffet just for them. A couple of guard rats kept the rest of the crowd away from them until they showed up. "This is wonderful!" exclaimed Betty. "Who do we owe for this treat?"

The stick bug Mom appeared at her shoulder and replied. "Well, we wanted to ensure everyone had some kind of little treat. You really have to thank Sniff and his rat sailors, though. One of his rats found this bunch just yesterday. Some human must have thought they weren't good to eat anymore and threw them out, but he knew you'd be happy so he grabbed them. Fortunately the stream was nearby so they just sailed up and back to get them."

Rawk, meanwhile, had remained in party mode ever since the wedding ceremony. Hanging out near a large bowl of fruit punch he had a hollowed out pineapple in his hand, filled with the punch and complete with a little umbrella in it. In his other hand he had the dreaded chicken hat and was waving it at everyone who came by for a drink.

"This is a no frown zone, everyone! Smiles only! I've had plenty more of these hats made up. You don't want to be wearing this all night!"

There seemed no danger of that actually happening. Even Checkers had mellowed as the dinner wore on. Groaning, he sat back and looked at his wife Rosie. "I can't eat another bite. I have to admit, they outdid themselves. And it really doesn't look like there was too much food."

Looking over at the buffet tables she had to agree, as the leftovers were looking pretty minimal. Even as she said it an army of Junk Town animals appeared as if on cue to pitch in and do clean up.

At the same time a growing frenzy of activity began in another part of the soccer field. Once again the stage was in place at one end and Twitch's Rabbit RawkStar band equipment had been set up on it but, oddly enough, the curtain usually drawn across the stage until show time wasn't set up there. Instead, the curious animals could see it was set up off to the side of the stage. A steady parade of engineer rabbits had made their way behind the mysterious curtain and could be heard bustling about. Anticipation for the show began to grow.

Some invisible signal was finally given and Rawk took the stage. "All right! We've got a special night ready for a special couple. Before we get this going I'd just like to thank all the performers and our rabbit friends for their help. It wouldn't happen without a bunch of party animals! And yes, this is a beach party! Let's go!"

As he finished the curtain was pulled aside and a small army of rabbits rushed forward pushing wheelbarrows filled with sand. Each load was dumped in a steady progression into the empty space between the stage area and the stands filled with animals. A group with makeshift rakes followed behind, spreading the piles of sand around to fill in the gaps.

But that was far from all. The crowd gaped in amazement as another group of rabbits began distributing big fake palm trees in little pots around the perimeter of the clearing. A big wooden sign made to look like driftwood was erected over it all that said 'Coconut Beach'. A few beach hammocks were strung between the fake trees for effect.

The big surprise was in the background, however. The engineer rabbits had gone all out this time, building a large artificial pool. A water mill scooped water from the stream and sent it along a little canal to the pool. A couple of fake shark fins sticking out of the water had been added for effect. Off to one side was a little wooden building with a sign that said 'Surf Shack'. Stacked beside it were several boogie boards for surfing. At the far end was a metal tower with a chair sticking out on a bar over the water that looked much like a lifeguard's chair.

Rawk got the party started with a few songs that soon had everyone dancing in their seats. Twitch and the RawkStars had obviously been practicing and were very good. He soon shifted to a stand up routine that had everyone alternately howling with laughter and groaning from a series of extremely bad puns and jokes.

"Okay, only one more for you," promised Rawk. "Did you hear about the wolf attack we had last week? Turned out to be a false alarm. Can you believe it? The wolves attacking were so dumb they left before the attack started. They heard dinner bells ringing!"

After several warnings he was about to get pounded with an avalanche of rotten fruit he finally turned the show over to a series of other performers. A motley group of cats and dogs led by Peter the Pig started the rest of show. The crowd howled with laughter as they realized the cats and dogs were wearing a clown costume of the same rainbow of color they'd applied to the wolves they'd caught. Peter, however, had voluntarily had himself actually painted just like the wolves. The monkeys followed Peter's dance routine with a stunning juggling routine.

Stepping to the front once again Rawk called for attention as a small group of rabbits began setting up two curious looking poles with a fork at the top of each and several notches set at regular intervals along their length. Once they'd set another pole across the top and stepped to the side Rawk addressed the crowd.

"Are we having fun? Yeah! Well, here's another one for you." Before continuing he raised a small trophy above his head for all to see. "So this is the first annual Limbo Champ Contest and this is the trophy. Who wants to be the first winner? How low can you go?!"

The competition was fierce as the pole was steadily lowered closer and closer to the ground, but the contest quickly came down to a struggle between a determined group of rats and the stick bugs. The bar got incredibly low and soon eliminated most of the competitors. The only two left were Sniff the rat and Twiggs the stick bug.

Sniff was good. He twisted himself in ways that made everyone gasp, all thinking he was going to injure himself for certain. With immense strength he beat the last effort of Twiggs and bounded up with fists raised to the cheers of his supporters.

Twiggs grimaced watching the rat. He gave it his best effort, but couldn't do it. The stick bug supporters groaned as he fell and the crowd of rats began to dance in their seats, certain of victory.

Rawk stepped forward once again, holding the trophy high. "How about it everyone? Anyone else want to try this? Last chance!"

"Yes!"

Everyone turned to find Windy standing in her seat, hand in the air for attention.

"Sure, come on down Windy," said Rawk.

"No, no, not me. Him!" Windy smiled sweetly and pointed at Sticks. "I'll bet he could take it lower!"

Sticks knew his jaw had dropped open as all eyes fell on him.

"Yeah!! Go get 'em, mate!" howled Wally. Several others in the crowd began chanting his name in encouragement.

With a quiet groan Sticks held up a hand to acknowledge the crowd. Knowing he wasn't getting out of this one he made his way to where Rawk and Sniff waited. Up close the limbo pole seemed even closer to the ground.

Taking a few moments to stretch his muscles, Sticks plotted his approach to it and began. With deliberate, slow effort he worked his way under the bar. He had one moment where he nudged the bar with his shoulder and it teetered back and forth. The crowd held its breath, but the bar slowly stopped and fell back into place. With a final victorious effort Sticks pulled himself to the other side of the bar and stood up.

Sniff just groaned and glared at Sticks as the crowd went wild. "You just had to make that, didn't you?" Sighing, the rat watched as the rabbit attendants moved the bar what looked like one impossible notch lower.

"You're up, Sniff," said Rawk. "Unless you want to forfeit?"

"As if," snorted the rat, glaring at Rawk. With a deep breath Sniff began working his way underneath the bar. At the mid point, though, it was clear he was struggling. Disaster finally struck as his muscles gave out and he collapsed onto his back with a groan.

"Right, over to you, Sticks," said Rawk.

"Must I?" groaned the stick bug. "Can't we just declare a tie?"

"Nope. Besides, listen to the crowd. They'll never forgive you."

Listening to the cheers Sticks sighed and stepped forward. With every muscle soon burning he slowly tackled the bar. Twice he almost fell and once he nudged the bar inadvertently, perilously close to knocking it off. But with one final, massive effort he pulled himself under the bar.

The roar of the crowd seemed endless. Sniff took a bow towards Sticks, acknowledging defeat. Rawk presented Sticks the trophy and held his other arm high. "Ladies and gentlemen, I give you your first limbo champ!"

As the cheers finally began to die off Rawk waved for attention. "Well, I hope you've all enjoyed the entertainment tonight. Congratulations once again to our newlyweds!" Wally and Leaf smiled and waved back.

"So before we get to the very last part of the show I have just a couple of things you need to know. We have several boogie boards over there for the kids to use in the pool our clever rabbit friends have built. Also, they'll be setting up a beach volleyball court off to the side over there for anyone who wants to put together some teams and have a go at each other. For those not into that the dance starts right after this next routine. Sound good?"

Making his way over to the pool, Rawk stepped up to the lifeguard structure the rabbits had built and climbed onto the seat hanging out over the water. As he did so several engineer rabbits strung a net up in the air beside him and attached a bar with a target board to the metal tower. All was finally revealed as another rabbit came forward and planted a large sign in the sand that said 'Dunk Tank'.

There was an immediate clamor as those quick enough to see what was coming rushed forward to line up for a chance to dunk the parrot. Sniff the rat beat them all and glared all around, defending his position first in line. "You're going down, bird. I've been waiting for an opportunity like this!"

"Right!" said Rawk. "So who says I don't have a sense of humor? Bring it on!"

***

Several dunks later the dance finally began. Wally and Leaf did their first dance to the cheers of the crowd. Sticks and Windy joined in next as part of the wedding party and soon after everyone else joined in.

Windy smiled up at Sticks as they danced. "I knew you could do it, you know."

"I thought you were cheering for Twiggs," said Sticks.

"I was. But I can cheer for you, too, can't I?"

Sticks just smiled. The dance ended and Wally came over for a dance with Windy. Seeing no one else to dance with Sticks wandered over to the punch bowl.

The party was only just starting. Rawk soon had a conga line snaking through the crowd while another bunch of animals had borrowed his supply of chicken hats and were doing an improvised chicken dance.

Over at the volleyball court a crowd was cheering on the participants. A large crowd of children had made themselves at home in the pool and were putting the boogie boards to good use. The rabbits had built a slide that landed anyone using it in the pool at its end and a large lineup soon formed of those waiting a turn. In between songs Twitch would regularly kick a few plastic beach balls they had found somewhere into the dancing crowd and soon they were bouncing everywhere.

Leaf found Sticks some time later still hanging out around the punch bowl, watching the crowd. Walking up she glared at him, hands on her hips. "What are you doing?"

Looking around in puzzlement, wondering if there was someone else she was talking to, Sticks finally realized it really was him she wanted. Worse, she didn't seem happy.

"Uh, what am I doing? Well, I'm standing here?"

"Of course you are, you fool. I can see that. What I want to know is why you aren't dancing with Windy?"

"Windy? Ah, I don't know?" Seeing her glare, he realized that answer wasn't what she wanted. "Okay, should I be?"

Leaf groaned. "How dense are you, anyway? Honestly, if everyone knew our Mayor was this thick there'd be a stampede to get you out of office. Of course you should be dancing with her!"

Leaf could see Sticks was baffled, so she groaned again. "What's holding you back?"

"Uhh," replied Sticks, finally finding his voice. "Well, I can't intrude. You know, I can't try and steal someone else's girl."

"What? Who?" A light dawned on Leaf's face, as she finally understood. "You mean Twiggs? Oh!!" Groaning again, she slapped her forehead and laughed. "Twiggs isn't her boyfriend, you dummy. He's her uncle! I know he doesn't look that old. He's the younger, much younger, brother of her Dad and she was the first child, so they aren't that far apart in age. They all got split up in the pet store long ago so Twiggs became her kind of default Dad. Dear brother, please pick your jaw up off the ground."

Sticks was in shock. "Oh. Ohh! So that means..."

"Yes, you imbecile. She doesn't have a boyfriend and, trust me, she really wants you to get over there and dance with her!"

***

Sticks was struggling as Leaf returned to Wally. A wild surge of hope was building within alongside the realization his sister was right, he had been a complete fool to make assumptions based on surface impressions. Shaking his head, he was about to begin looking for Windy when a sudden inspiration struck and he walked off into the distance.

Leaf, now back with Wally, could only stare in exasperation as she watched him walk away. "Now what is he doing? I don't believe it!" She was about to go after him again, but Wally stopped her.

"Hang on, love. He may have been off the mark till now, but I have confidence. He's got something in mind."

Sure enough, Sticks returned a little later and began making his way over to where Windy was sitting watching the dancers go by. Wally started laughing as he saw Sticks was carrying a ring of flowers strung together in one hand and one of Rawk's chicken hats in the other. "Ha! Told you! Our Mayor is on the job now. Watch this!" chuckled Wally.

Windy saw him coming and stood up, her eyes crinkling in puzzlement seeing what he was bringing.

"Hello, Windy," said Sticks, coming to a stop in front of her.

"Hi," she replied, looking deliberately at what he had in his hands. "I'm not sure if those are for me, but if they are I'd prefer the flowers! I don't do chicken hats."

"Huh, yes, the flowers are for you, if you'll have them."

"Sure! Why wouldn't I want them?" she asked, smiling in puzzlement again.

Lifting them over her head and arranging them around her neck he explained how he'd misunderstood her relationship with Twiggs. "So the flowers are to say I'm sorry. As for me, well, you see what a fool I've been and how I deserve to be punished accordingly. A chicken hat is the closest thing I can find resembling a dunce cap so it'll have to do."

Arranging it on his head, he smiled hopefully at Windy. "Now we've got that sorted out, I'm wondering if you could see your way clear to dancing with a fool in a chicken hat?"

Windy doubled over in laughter. Finally catching her breath, she looked at him with shining eyes. "I'll dance all night with you!" Taking his arm she gave him a kiss and led him into the crowd of dancers.

They were soon lost in the dance with eyes only for each other, which is why they never saw what was happening around them. As the final notes of the song were played they realized the dancers around them had all backed away and they were in the center of a huge circle of watching animals.

With a start they both looked around in puzzlement, wondering what was happening. The crowd saw Windy and Sticks were finally aware of them and they began cheering and applauding loudly as one. Both stick bugs blushed and gave the watching animals sheepish grins.

Sticks looked at Windy and shrugged. "I guess we should give them something to really cheer about." Pulling her close he gave her a long kiss. The crowd roared even louder.

Chapter Eight

Life slowly returned to normal in Junk Town. Everyone slept in late the next few days as the crowds of forest animals that had come for the party went their separate ways. The cleanup took a few days, but no one was in a rush. Sticks and Twitch knew the animals had all worked at a hard pace to make it all happen, so everyone appreciated a few slower days.

The warm days had stretched into the beginning of July, with little rain to moderate the heat. The children of Junk Town had no complaints, as the pool the rabbit engineers had built was still in full operation.

Even better, they'd somehow found the time to add a new feature. A small hand operated pump had been found in the junkyard and connected to a hose drawing water from the pool. Another hose was attached to the top of a pole for the output, spraying water in a wide pattern. With a willing adult to do the pumping the children could run back and forth under the spray and splash about.

"Come on kids! Time for a shower!" called Peter the pig, who was the happy volunteer. The new water feature resulted in several large puddles forming in the area around it and he spent most of his day wallowing in the mud to stay cool when he wasn't working the pump. Everyone could see the pig suffered in the heat and had little energy to do much else.

Knowing that was where he preferred to be was actually convenient for the Junk Town animals.

Sticks had resumed worrying about whether another attack could be in the offing. Being at the pool made Peter the perfect choice for guard over the crowd of playing children, freeing the adults to work at whatever needed doing.

When the next attack came they had reason to be glad he was there. The Junk Town animals were also fortunate they had sharp-eyed border guards posted. One of them at a distant post spotted a very large group of wolves trying to sneak past the Junk Town defenses in single file. The wolves were already congratulating themselves as they wound their way forward, as it seemed their patient gathering of intelligence on where the traps had been laid was paying off.

With the alarm given, a crowd of Junk Town animals came rushing to the defense. Soon a hail of rocks was pounding the wolves still forced into a single file formation as they tried to wind their way through the traps. In the distance past the border of Junk Town a frustrated group of wolves were milling about, waiting their turn.

Because the wolves were forced into single file it meant the defenders could concentrate their fire on one wolf at a time. The resulting barrage was impossible to withstand and the wolves trying to work their way through were forced to a standstill. Two of them stumbled off the path through the traps and ended up in them. The Junk Town defenders cheered as the wolves trying to get through began to stumble back the way they came, frustrated at their defeat.

The Junk Town defenses, however, hadn't been fully set in place when the first two wolves had come to the attack. Even as the others were being driven back, these two finally got past the series of traps they knew were in place. That, however, didn't win them much.

A virtual forest of spears was waiting for them. Sticks stepped forward and just glared for a long moment at the two wolves as they searched in desperation for a way around the spears.

"Come on guys, you know you're not going to get past us and we sharpened our spears just for this kind of occasion. So why don't you just turn around and go back the way you came?"

One of the wolves snarled in response while the other laughed. "No, I don't think so, bug. We're only just getting started!" As he said it new warnings were shouted from two different locations on the border. Two new attempts to sneak past the traps were underway, while three wolves had already been caught in new traps the wolf spies hadn't found.

The Junk Town defenders were ready for them. Sticks had long planned for the possibility of attacks on a wide front and he quickly dispatched groups of defenders to deal with each new approach of the wolves. The voice of Twitch intruded on his thoughts as he did.

"Sticks? We've got this under control, but where are the crows? I don't see any of them anywhere. I don't like this."

With a quick look around, Sticks realized he was right. "Yes, that's not good. Have you heard anything from the guards on the other side of town yet?"

Even as he spoke, a warning signal came. A large group of crows, tightly bunched in formation flew over the far border of town in a rush. With a chill running down his spine, Sticks saw exactly where the birds were headed and finally understood the strategy the predators were using.

"The children! Twitch, they're after the kids!" With sickening certainty Sticks knew they couldn't possibly get there in time to defend the large crowd of children only now finally all out of the pool and massing together to run and hide. With the children under attack the temptation of the parents to rush to their aid would be overwhelming. All the discipline and drills they'd practiced would be for nothing if the Junk Town defenders broke ranks. Sticks knew it would turn into mass confusion if he couldn't stop it.

Sticks sent a group of defenders with slingshots rushing to take on the crows even as the children cowered in fear and stopped where they were. Frozen with fear seeing the pack of crows diving to the attack the children clustered together trying to find safety in numbers. The lead crows realized they had one defender to contend with, but smiled when they saw it was only Peter the pig.

Peter wasn't smiling back. Making himself as big as possible and stamping back and forth in front of the children he bared his teeth at the crows. With an immense leap the pig shocked the very lead crow, catching him by the leg with his teeth as the crow flew by. Yanked out of the air the crow had time for a surprised squawk before Peter smashed him hard face first into the ground.

The following crows, expecting an easy time of it, were shocked at the outcome and tried too late to slow up. Leaving the first crow lying in a crumpled heap trying to gather his wits Peter grabbed a second crow and did the same to him.

By this time the rest had seen enough and were trying to keep Peter at a healthy distance. "Come on, take on someone your own size you cowards!" Peter snarled at the crows, trying to goad them into coming after him. "Thought I was a pushover, didn't you? Attack my herd, will you? If I catch you you're going to pay big time!"

The crows didn't take the bait because with their numbers they didn't have to. Encircling the frightened children and the pig, the crows began darting in two and three at a time to try and snatch a child while the pig was occupied elsewhere.

Peter was heroic in defense. He seemed tireless, moving faster than anyone had ever seen him in a whirlwind of flashing teeth and hooves, arriving wherever the need was greatest. The crows found opportunities to peck and claw at him and did so with glee, knowing he couldn't possibly keep it up. But he didn't need to as help finally arrived.

A howling wave of Junk Town animals smashed into the crows with an overwhelming fury. Knowing they were defending their children lent them a desperate strength that wasn't to be denied. Several crows were simply grabbed right out of the air and immediately surrounded by a crowd of angry animals pounding them into unconsciousness. Others were brought down in a crushing hail of rocks from all directions. Those caught on the ground were hit on the head with sticks from several different directions at once.

Not one crow was left standing. A pile of over two dozen injured and still unconscious crow prisoners was built as Twitch the rabbit came over to Peter. "Well done! I don't know how we can repay you for this. We thought the children were goners!"

Peter was still flushed and wheezing from the effort. "Well, they're the herd's children. I had to! And I'm glad you got here when you did," he finally gasped out. "I couldn't have kept that up much longer."

With the crows no longer a threat Twitch sent a large number of the animals back to help the tiring defenders still struggling with the wolves. They arrived just in time, as the wolves were now pressing in on several fronts. The extra help meant the rabbits now had time to bring their big slingshot into play and soon huge rocks were flying over the heads of the defenders, smashing into the wolves with crushing effect.

The wolves countered by calling up reserves. Another group of crows came to the attack in a rush over the heads of the wolves in a move calculated to bring dismay to the struggling defenders. They were as large as the group that attacked the children, and they were soon diving and snapping at everyone in reach.

The sudden thunder of a large diesel engine firing to life in the distance stopped both attackers and defenders alike in their tracks. Turning to find the source, they realized the sound was coming from the direction of the road to the city by the entrance to Junk Town. The sound grew to a steady, frightening roar and as it did a harsh, metallic clanking noise could be heard. Unable to see what it was, the animals all shrunk back in fear at the overwhelming, brutal power of the sound.

Sticks was the first to recover, realizing the more immediate threat was still the wolves in front of them. One by one, however, they began to slink away, ears flattened in fear at the sound. The crows took flight too, gathering in a large cluster and heading back to the forest.

Still trying to process what was happening Sticks suddenly realized the wolf nearest to him was lingering. Looking closer he saw he was wearing a leather collar with bells. With sudden insight he recognized the young wolf he'd talked to before.

As the wolf turned to go Sticks called out to him. "Hey! It doesn't have to be this way! Remember?"

The wolf stopped, an anguished look on his face. Sticks held his gaze on the wolf for a long moment, before the wolf finally hung his head and turning, was gone like the others.

Sticks had no more time to devote to the predators. Issuing orders for everyone to hide Sticks led a small group of animals over to the old humans trailer and peeked around the corner. Twitch and several of the other animal leaders joined him.

What they found chilled everyone with fear. The humans had returned to Junk Town once again, but none of the animals had ever seen these ones. Worse, they had brought some very frightening machines with them.

A large flatbed trailer truck was now parked on the road in front of the entrance to Junk Town. Three human males wearing hard hats could be seen. One had opened the lock on the chain across the entrance and had pulled it to the side so the way in was clear.

Making the frightening noise was a huge bulldozer with an enormous blade on the front being driven by another one of the men. The harsh clanking sound the animals had heard was the noise made by the tracks of the bulldozer as they rotated on the metal wheels. As the animals watched the man finished driving the machine off the bed of the trailer and headed over to the entrance to Junk Town.

The third man was seated on yet another machine on the bed of the truck. Seeing the way was now clear he started his machine and it too came to life with its own frightening roar of sound. This was a different machine, however. Instead of metal tracks this machine had large, hard rubber wheels and on the front instead of a blade it had a huge metal bucket. This was a front-end loader, a much more flexible and easier to move machine.

The man driving the bulldozer pulled up and leaned over to speak to the man standing on the ground by the entrance. "Where do you want me to park it, boss? It doesn't look to me like there'll be much room to maneuver when we've got both of these in there."

The man on the ground nodded agreement and massaged his chin with one hand, studying the area in front of the old humans trailer. "Yeah, you're right. See that big pile of old metal car parts over there? Why don't you just shove it back about fifty feet? That should do it, I think. Just park it there once you've cleared the space. I'll get Tom to park the loader beside you."

Coming to clanking life once again, the man drove the bulldozer over to the pile of junk the man had indicated. Reaching the pile the machine's thunder reached a truly frightening new height, as the man worked the hard blade and shoved the heavy pile of junk to where he wanted it. The machine's brute, unstoppable strength chilled the watching animals as in very little time the machine had cleared a large new space with frightening ease. With job done the man backed the bulldozer into the space and turned the machine off.

His companion with the front-end loader had meanwhile driven his machine off the truck and was waiting for the bulldozer to finish its work. Driving over he parked the loader beside it and turned his machine off too. The sudden silence was delightful, but the animals were too frightened to enjoy it. By now virtually all of the Junk Town animals had crept into positions where they could remain hidden but still see what was happening.

The two men driving the machines climbed down and joined the third. All three took a moment to look around, before one finally spoke up. "This place is huge. Looks like a big job."

"Hmm," replied the man called the boss, taking his time to study his surroundings again. "I don't think it'll take us that long once we get going. If the trucks stay on schedule we'll be fine. Well, that's for next week anyway. Come on, guys. Lets go enjoy our weekend."

Turning, all three left and headed for the now empty flatbed truck still sitting on the road. Stopping only briefly to pull the chain across and lock the entrance to Junk Town once again, they got in the truck and drove away.

As a real silence finally descended the animals gradually came out of hiding. The crowd gathered on the ground in front of the hulking machines that loomed over them. No one said anything for several long moments.

As he knew they would, the crowd seemed to turn as one and look at Sticks. Sticks could only heave a deep sigh. "I know what you're thinking everyone, and the answer is I have no idea what this means."

The comment brought another long silence to the crowd, until Oscar the cat broke it with a grim smile. "Well, I may end up wearing a chicken hat tonight for saying this, but I'm thinking this just can't be good. The last time humans showed up without warning here they hauled Stuff away on us."

His small attempt to bring a little humor to the situation didn't work, as the frightened crowd could only grimace in response. The frowns stayed in place as a group of crows sitting in the trees high above the crowd suddenly made their presence known by cawing with harsh laughter. The misery of the Junk Town animals was complete.

Chapter Nine

Dinner around the fire that night was a subdued affair with many animals sunk deep in thought. Sticks and Twitch had debriefed several animals on what happened and now had a fuller understanding of what they'd faced that day.

In truth both had to acknowledge the intrusion of the humans was a blessing in disguise. The predators had attacked with a clear plan and overall strategy. The initial attack by the wolves was clearly just a distraction, as was the attack on the children. Both Sticks and Twitch realized the real attack was what they had been facing when the humans had arrived on the scene. They also both strongly felt the predators had even come prepared with yet another surprise that they hadn't been able to spring on the Junk Town defenders. In short, the predators had adapted their strategy and had been executing a carefully planned attack.

"I still think we could have held them off, Sticks," said Twitch. "The problem is the crows. Aside from our artillery, we have no defense against them flying around. It's too bad we couldn't convince the eagles to join us."

Rawk was nearby and overheard Twitch. Sitting up in sudden surprise, he looked hard at the two Junk Town leaders.

"Yeah, we could really use them!" replied Sticks. "But even so there aren't enough of them to go around. I agree, the crows obviously spied out our defenses and told the wolves all about them."

"Hey, guys, something just occurred to me. I know where there are more eagles," said Rawk. "There were some others hanging around at that place where our eagle friends were staying when I found them. I couldn't talk our friends into moving here, but maybe I could recruit some others?"

Twitch and Sticks looked at each other and then back at the parrot. "Sure Rawk, we'll take all the help we can get," said Twitch.

Turning back to Sticks, he continued their conversation. "Anyway, we still have a few tricks to play and I don't think... no, I know they don't know about all of them. Our monkey friends also suggested something we hadn't thought of that might help against the birds, too. The real question is what are we going to do about the humans?"

Sticks could only shrug. "I wish I knew more about what's going on. Hard to make a plan to counter something when you don't know what you're fighting. It's obvious those machines are here to do something and we have to assume we may not like it. But I have no idea how to stop them."

"Wolves are powerful and hard to defend against, but we're managing," said Leaf, joining the conversation. "We can't give up without trying."

"Of course not," replied Sticks. "I guess I'm just saying we've got to find out more. I don't know how we're going to do that, but that's the job. As for those machines, well, I will confess I'm scared we still won't have a way to stop them even if we do know what's happening."

"Ah, well, my gang of crazy engineers may be able to help with that," said Twitch, a tiny smile creasing his face. "Might not help for long, but we do have something I think we can try if we have to."

"What about the female human that showed up, Sticks? She had to have been the old human's daughter. Maybe she'll come back and help us?" said Leaf.

Sticks could only shrug once again. "Maybe. We can't count on it. We're just going to have to adapt to whatever happens."

***

Leaf's comment at dinner came true, at least in part.

The next day the ears of the wary animals all perked up the instant the sound of two cars pulling up at the entrance to Junk Town came. By the time the animals found places to watch what was happening while staying hidden the gate had been unlocked and both cars were being parked in front of the old human's trailer.

The first car held a single occupant. This was a man about the same age as the woman that had come to Junk Town earlier. He was wearing rough work clothes. He got out, looking around with a curious look on his face, and went over to join the occupants of the second car. A woman and two young children stepped out to meet him. The Junk Town animals immediately recognized her as the woman that had visited on her own several weeks before. The two children were a boy and a girl and looked to be about the same age, perhaps seven or eight years old.

The man came over and shook the woman's hand. "Well, it's been a while since I've been here, but it doesn't look like things have changed much."

"I expect not," replied the woman, who turned and gestured at the two children. "These are my kids, Sarah and Charlie. They're out of school for the summer."

The man smiled at them, then turned back to the woman. "Well, shall we?"

"Let's go. Come on kids."

The little group left their cars and walked off into the junkyard. The man pulled out a notebook and stopped them by each pile of different junk to make notes. Almost two hours later they finally returned to the old humans trailer.

By this time the children were completely bored and were fidgeting enough to annoy their mother. "Can you two settle down please?"

"Can we go play, mom?" said the boy. "I'm tired of walking around. I'd like to go look at the machines."

The woman sighed. "Fine. Just stay in sight, please. You two stay with each other and don't wander off."

The children immediately ran over to where the two machines were parked and began climbing them. One went to each machine and sat in the driver's seat, completely dwarfed by the size of the machine. Both were soon lost in fantasies they were driving the monster machines wherever they wanted to go.

Both adults turned from watching the children to look at each other once again. "Well? Have you got what you need?" said the woman with a tired sigh.

"Uh, yeah, I think so," said the man with a last look at his notebook. "The only place we haven't checked out is this back corner behind the trailer. Is there any stuff I could use there?"

"Well, I don't think so, but lets go look," replied the woman as they both walked around the corner of the trailer.

Stopping short in surprise the man looked around at the expanse of Junk Town. Looking over at the woman with raised eyebrows he chuckled. "What's all this?"

The woman shrugged her shoulders. "I have no idea what this is or what he was doing. Weird, isn't it? It's all just junk, but it seems organized. Well, my Dad had problems, right? It all probably made some kind of strange sense to him."

"Huh. Yeah, he was an odd bird sometimes, but I liked him!" Walking further into Junk Town the man headed for the old barn in the far corner. "I just want to check this out, see if there's anything usable inside," he called over his shoulder to the woman, who remained standing where she was.

Sticks and Twitch and the rest of the animals were on edge, trying to understand what the two humans were talking about. "Well, what do you think?" said Twitch, nudging Sticks and pointing over to where the two children were still playing on the machines. "Maybe we can get some information from them?"

"Let's try it. It's the first opportunity we've had to talk to them when the adults aren't around. Why don't you and some of your rabbits approach them? You won't look threatening and they probably won't raise a fuss that would bring their mother running. I'll stay here and keep listening in."

Nodding agreement Twitch signaled two of his rabbits to follow him and headed for the children. The girl was the first to see them and she squealed with delight, alerting her brother. "Charlie! Look! Those are rabbits, aren't they?"

The boy was equally fascinated. "Wow! They are! And they don't look frightened of us either. Lets see if they'll let us get close."

Climbing down from the machines the two children approached the rabbits slowly. The three rabbits sat in a group watching them come nearer until Twitch finally broke the silence. "Hello! Welcome to Junk Town! My name is Twitch."

The two children looked at each other and smiled. "Hi! Uh, it's nice to meet you. I'm Sara and this is Charlie. What are you doing here?" asked the girl.

Twitch smiled back. "Well, we live here. Actually, we were hoping to ask you the same question."

"Kids! Come on, let's go!" called their mother. "We're almost done for today!"

Twitch looked over his shoulder and saw both adults returning to the cars. "Are you coming back tomorrow?"

"Yes, that's what Mom said," replied the boy.

"We'll find you tomorrow then," said Twitch. Turning, the three rabbits dashed for cover.

The two children looked at each other in puzzlement and then obediently went to their mother. The little girl tugged at her mother's hand just as she was about to say something to the man. "Mom! We found some rabbits living here."

The woman gave her daughter a distracted glance. "Yes, honey, I'm not surprised. There's probably lots of animals around here."

The man was finishing making some final notes in his book. Closing it with a snap he put it under his arm and put away his pen. "Okay. I think that's it."

"So you're sure you can take it all?" asked the woman.

"Yeah, pretty much. He added a few things from the last time I was here, but it's more or less what I remembered. You can tell the guys on Monday to just load it all up. With all this stuff I'll have the biggest junkyard in town! It's a good thing I have the space for it. The only exception is this trailer and the barn and all that stuff out back, of course."

"You don't know anyone who might want the buildings?"

The man grimaced. "Not really. They're pretty old and beat up. It would take a lot to make them more presentable. I'm thinking they could have rot in more than a few spots, too. You could try placing an ad. You never know who might find a use for them."

"Right. Well, I was expecting that. I may just get them to haul it all away too once I'm done with it. Anyway, thanks for everything!"

"Hey, thank you. I think this is a good deal for both of us. See you later." Hopping in his car, the man drove away.

Heaving a big sigh of relief the woman opened the doors of the car for the children and they climbed in. "Mom, what was that all about?" asked the little girl.

"Hmm?" she replied, starting the car. "The man? Oh, he's buying all of the junk here for his own junkyard. He already had a pretty good idea of what was here because he knew your grandpa, but he had to check it out. They're coming to start hauling all the junk away on Monday morning."

The girl was concerned. "What about the rabbits that live there, Mom?"

"Rabbits? Don't worry about them, honey. I'm sure they'll be fine. You can look for them again tomorrow." Stopping to lock the gate, the woman and children drove away.

***

They were a frustrated and worried lot that night.

Twitch was kicking himself for not getting more information from the children. Sticks and the rest of the animals consoled him as best they could by assuring him there simply had not been enough time.

The troubling part was the conversation between the man and woman right before they left. The rabbit engineers in particular were almost frantic with concern. They had become so dependent on the junkyard as a source of material they could use for their own creative purposes they could not see how they could function without it.

The animals were feeling so down there wasn't even any talk of getting out the chicken hat. "We'll just have to see what tomorrow brings," said Sticks with a shrug.

Chapter Ten

The Junk Town animals were a tired lot the next day. No one had slept well, worried as they all were about their future. The daily routine of life in Junk Town had to carry on, though, and everyone went to forage for breakfast as usual.

The woman and the two children returned just as many had finished. After parking the car the woman went to the trailer and opened the door. The children followed behind and they all disappeared inside.

They weren't inside for long. The door burst open and the little girl ran outside sneezing several times in succession. The woman appeared with the boy in tow and looked at both children.

"Sorry, honey, I guess it's too dusty in here for you. Why don't you two just play in the junkyard? I've got work to do in here."

"Okay, mom," snuffled the girl. "I'm sorry, I wanted to help you, but it makes my nose tickle in there."

"It's all right. Just stay close and stay out of trouble. I'm going to be in here for a while." Turning, she went back inside the trailer.

The boy and girl looked around the junkyard and then turned to look at each other. "Want to go play on the machines again?" asked the boy.

"Why don't we try to find the rabbits again?" countered the girl.

"Sure. They ran off behind the trailer yesterday so lets start there." Turning, they walked around the corner of the trailer and began to poke about.

The wary Junk Town animals were all in hiding, of course. Seeing it was only the children Twitch and Sticks looked at each other and, taking a deep breath together, stepped into view. "Hello again!" said Twitch.

The two children looked to see where the voice had come from and their eyes lit up with interest as they saw the two animals. Walking over to where Sticks and Twitch waited the two children glanced at Twitch before settling their gaze on Sticks.

"Uh, hello again, Twitch," said Charlie, with a quick look at the rabbit. "We're sorry we couldn't stay to talk to you yesterday." Unable to contain his curiosity any longer, he looked deliberately at Sticks. "Who's your friend? I've never seen a bug like him before."

"This is the Mayor of Junk Town. His name is Sticks, which is probably a good name for a stick bug."

"Mayor?" said Sarah.

"Yes, that's what they wanted me to be," replied Sticks with a smile. "Would you like a tour? You can meet the rest of the animals that live here."

An hour later the children found themselves sitting near the fire pit surrounded by a host of Junk Town animals. A few of the little stick bugs were crawling on the arms of the children. Both the human children and the stick bugs were equally fascinated with each other.

"So you see, we've all done the best we could to make a home here because we had nowhere else to go and we could defend ourselves better by working together," said Sticks, finishing his explanation of what they were doing here.

The children looked troubled. "Do you get attacked often?"

"Sure. We had a really big attack just the other day." As Sticks gave the details of what had happened the children's faces fell even further. "So this is why we really wanted to meet you. We've been happy here in Junk Town, but there's obviously something going on. We heard the man and your mother talking yesterday and it sounds like they're going to take all the junk away. Is that all that's happening?"

The two children looked hard at each other and then back at the nervous crowd of animals. "We don't know," replied Sarah, a look of unease on her face. "Mom hasn't told us much. We had to tag along with her because there's no one to watch over us. We know she's going through the things in Grandpa's trailer for anything she wants to keep, but once she's done I think we'll be going home again."

One of the rabbit moms, clutching a little one in her arms, spoke up. "Can you find out more for us? We need to know if we have to find a new home."

"Sure. Charlie, lets go ask mom. We'll be back."

High in the trees nearby and well hidden, the two watching crows settled in for a long wait.

Their leader Spike had told them they would need patience to get the information he wanted.
***

Their mother was still working her way through the huge piles of junk her father had collected over the years and was only half listening as the children asked her what was going on.

"Hmm? Oh, sorry kids. I'll stop for a moment. I need a break anyway. What did you want?"

"We're wondering what's happening here. The man that was here yesterday is going to take away all the junk, right?"

"Yes. That's why the bulldozer and the front-end loader are here. The men will be here tomorrow morning to start hauling it away."

"So what happens then, Mom? Are we moving in here?" asked the boy.

"Moving in?" laughed his mother. "Whatever gave you that idea? No, that's definitely not going to happen. I spent enough time here when I was your age and I certainly don't want to go back in time."

"Okay, so are we going to leave the rest of this as it is?"

"No, that's not happening either. I have to figure out what to do with this trailer and that junk in the back yard, but after that we're done here. The whole place has been sold, my dear."

"Sold?" chorused both children at the same time, looks of concern on their faces.

"Sure. The land here is very valuable now. When your Grandpa bought this it was a long way from the city and didn't cost much. The city has grown a lot over the years and is much closer now. A developer wanted me to sell it to him so they can build a new suburb for the city, so I did. We just have to clean the property up and we're done with it. I don't know, I may just get them to haul all this other stuff away too and get this over with. Just think, kids, we'll be so much better off. We'll be able to travel a bit and maybe buy a little house for ourselves."

The children looked at each other and then at their mother. "Mom, there's all kinds of animals live here. What will they do?" asked the boy in a worried voice.

Their mother had already turned her mind back to her task, however. "I'm sure they'll be fine. There's plenty of forest here for them to live in."

"But Mom, I don't think the forest is a very safe place..."

"Kids! Look, I'm sorry, I want to get as much done today as possible. We can't do anything about the forest animals. The city is getting bigger and bigger every day and you can't stop it. Sooner or later this place would've been developed and made part of the city. The animals will just have to adapt and move somewhere else. Now please go to the car, there's a lunch for each of you there. Please eat them and let me finish here. I think I only need another hour and I'll be done for today."

With little choice the children did as they were told. Carrying their lunches with them they went back to where the Junk Town animals were waiting. The glum looks on the faces of the two children told the animals it wasn't good news.

The animals were stunned. "Sold?" cried several when the children broke the news. All eyes turned to Sticks in desperate hope he could reassure them this wasn't happening.

He couldn't do that, though. Sticks felt as if the ground underneath his feet had turned to jelly and he had to sit down. After thinking for a moment, he looked back at the children. "When is this happening?"

The children looked at each other before the girl responded. "Mom said the junk is being hauled away starting tomorrow. She's still working her way through Grandpa's stuff in the trailer, but I don't think that will take her much longer. She has to decide what to do with the trailer and the barn and all of your homes and then she's done. She said the property has already been sold so I imagine it will happen soon. I think she's going to have the men haul this all away too."

Sticks sighed and looked at Twitch in desperation. "We need time. We can't just build another Junk Town somewhere else overnight."

"No, we certainly can't," replied Twitch. Turning, Twitch looked at a big group of rabbit engineers sitting nearby. "I think we'd better try that idea to see if we can buy some time. You should maybe get started on that now."

Without a word they got up and left as Twitch turned back to the children. "We've really found it useful to be living in a junkyard. I know all the junk here is being moved to another big junkyard. Do you know where it is?" The children shook their heads, so Twitch continued. "Do you think you could ask your Mom?"

"That would be great, Twitch, but it would be even better if we knew exactly when we have to be out of here," said Leaf.

The children saw the worry on the faces of the animals and agreed to try and help. Slowly finishing their lunches, the children and the Junk Town animals settled into a dispirited silence. Getting up to go back to the trailer and try talking to their mother once more, the children reassured the animals they would do their best.

The attack came just as they began to walk away. A faint squeal of surprise instantly cut off made them all turn to the direction of the sound. Two crows had swooped in fast and one had successfully snatched a rabbit child that had strayed a little ways from its mother. The approach had been undetected with everyone so distracted. A second child barely missed being grabbed by the other crow.

The Junk Town defenders immediately sent a hail of rocks in their direction, but it was far too late. The crow with the rabbit was already much too far away. The second settled on a perch just out of range and began cawing with cold laughter as the rabbit mother wailed in dismay.

"Well, sounds like Junk Town has a problem! I think I'll just pass this information on to Scar and Spike. See you soon!" Cawing again, he lifted off and flew after the other crow.

The two children were stunned. "That's awful!" cried the girl. "Does that happen often?"

"Far too often," said Leaf.

"Who is Scar? And Spike?" asked the boy. "What was that all about?"

As Sticks explained the two children were horrified and their face's faces grew even longer than before. Sticks turned to Twitch and sighed. "Well, we're going to have to come up with something here real fast. I don't know if they'll work up the courage to attack while those machines are here, but we can't assume they will hold back."

"Charlie, we've got to try and help them!"

"Yes! Let's go talk to Mom again."

This time they weren't walking. Running hard they were soon back in the trailer where they found their mother coming out of a back room with a box full of things. Walking right past the two children she ignored their cries for attention and put it down just outside the front door where two other boxes were already stacked. "Good, I was just about to call you. I've had enough of this for today. I just need to put these boxes in the car and lock up and we can go."

"Mom!" the children cried together, tugging at her arm.

"What?"

"The animals here are in trouble! We saw a crow carry off a rabbit child. They have nowhere to go. We can't let the predators get them!" cried the girl.

The woman heaved a great sigh and bent over to give the children both a hug. "Look, kids. I know you want to help them and I'm proud of you for that. But these are wild animals and they have predators. That's life in the forest and we can't change that. Okay? All right, it's time to leave. Help me carry these boxes to the car."

"But Mom, I don't think these are all wild animals. Maybe some of them are, I don't know. They said they were abandoned."

"Oh, honey, how would you know that? What an imagination. Look, even if they were abandoned they're in the wild now, aren't they?"

"Mom?" interrupted the girl. "How long before the new owner takes over here?"

"Well, officially that's another week away, but the junk will all be gone in a couple of days. I've decided to get them to just bulldoze this trailer and the barn down and haul it all off to the dump. So that means I'll be turning this over to the new owner probably in a couple of days. Satisfied?"

Without waiting for a response she picked up a box and headed for the car. "Let's go, kids. We'll be back here tomorrow morning to meet the men that'll haul everything away. You can play with your animal friends one more time then."

The children stood looking after her in frustration. A resigned look came over the boys face and he turned to his sister. "Quick, I'll help her with the boxes. I don't think she saw you bring your lunch kit back. Run back with it and tell the animals what we learned. I'll keep her busy and tell her you've forgotten your kit and have gone to get it."

Without a word, the girl turned and ran out of sight around the trailer. The animals gathered in anticipation as she ran up and explained what had happened.

"I'm sorry!" she cried. "We tried to convince her to help but she won't listen." The faces fell on the few animals that had held out hope the children could stop what was happening. As the girl explained her mother's decision to bulldoze their homes several animals gasped out loud.

The girl's heart broke watching the hope turn to disappointment on the faces of the animals. "I'm so sorry!" she wailed. "We'll keep trying. Mom said we'd be back in the morning. We'll try to find you as soon as we can."

Twitch stopped the girl just as she turned to run back to the car. "Please," he begged. "See if you can find out where the junk is being taken and how to get there. Maybe we can find our way to the new junkyard and make that our home."

"I will!" cried the girl before running hard back the way she came.

The Junk Town animals stared after her for a long while. Several hung their heads in dismay. A few snuffles could be heard as parents did their best to try and comfort the scared children.

Chapter Eleven

They were a gloomy bunch sitting around the fire that night after dinner.

Rawk did his best to try and cheer everyone up, but his audience was too distracted with worry. The parrot finally slumped into his chair near the fire in resignation. With a big sigh, he pulled out the chicken hat and put it on his head. The irony of it got him his biggest laughs of the night, although they didn't last long.

"Rawk, what are you putting that on for?" asked Windy. "None of this is your fault."

"Yeah, I know," replied the bird with a grimace. "I guess I'm just desperate for a laugh. Sort of like we all are right now. Ah, I'm sorry. Frustrated is a better word for it. Maybe I actually deserve to wear this thing."

"Well, it does suit you," laughed Sticks, walking into their midst with Twitch close behind. "Okay, everyone, listen up. Twitch and I have been inspecting our little surprise for tomorrow and we think it will work. It may not slow them down for very long, but it's a start. What we need to do now is settle on a plan." Seeing he had their attention, he gave them a grim smile in return.

"You don't really think we're just going to roll over and give in, do you? I don't intend to. So, here it is. The rabbits really, really want to have access to materials they can work with for our defenses. Our preferred plan is therefore to find out where this other junkyard is and make our way there. If we can't convince the owner to let us have some space we can at least set up right beside it in the forest. Either way, we'll get what we need."

"Sticks?" called one of the rats. "What if it's too far away? And how will we get there? The predators will certainly try to attack while we're traveling there, won't they?"

Sticks sighed. "All good questions. Yes, we'll be exposed to them while traveling for sure and we will be walking. There is no other way. I won't lie to you, we'll do our best to defend everyone, but it is likely we're going to have attacks along the way."

Sniff the rat stepped forward and Sticks looked at him, knowing he wanted to speak. "Sounds kind of risky to me. But you said this was the preferred plan. What will we do if that doesn't work for some reason? Like maybe this other place is an impossible distance away?"

Sticks looked at Twitch, who promptly grimaced and stepped forward to reply. "Ah, well, this isn't what I would call a good option, but it might buy us a little more time to figure out something better. The alternative plan is to try and build a new home close to the garbage dump."

Several animals groaned openly and Sniff snorted in disgust. "Great," said the rat. "You want us to move right next door to the smelliest place around. How is that a good idea?"

"Like I said, not a good option. I know it's smelly. There are all kinds of seagulls flying around who would be happy to attack us, too. Look, we need material to work with to build defenses and homes. The dump at least has the benefit of being relatively near our current home and there'll be some stuff to work with."

Sticks sighed as a silence descended on the crowd. "Hey, everyone, if there's a better idea please speak up."

No one did and this time the silence deepened. Sniff the rat finally lifted his head and turned to the crowd. "Guess we don't have much choice, do we? The only other option I see here is we all go our separate ways. At least some of us might escape the predators. Anyone for that idea?"

Several animals looked around at each other, troubled looks on their faces. Finally, one of the cat sisters spoke up in response. "I can't speak for anyone else here, but I've gotten used to having you all around. You don't really think that's a good idea, do you?"

"Nope," replied Sniff in a firm tone. "I just wanted to find out where everyone stands here. How about it, does everyone want to stick together? Hands up if that's what you want."

A forest of hands shot up in response, bringing a smile to the rats face. "Excellent!" he said, turning to face Sticks and Twitch. "Looks like we need to talk about a defensive plan for when we're on the move."

Sticks and Twitch smiled in relief at each other. "Well, we've already got a plan for that. Unfortunately, I think it's going to be a couple of days before we're ready. The rabbits are trying hard to build some carts we can pull. We'll fill them with food, spare spears and slingshots. It's too dark to work on all this now so we'll have to be at it when dawn comes tomorrow. So relax for tonight everyone and be ready for tomorrow."

The effect on the Junk Town animals was startling. The tension and worry still filled the air, but a light had returned to the faces of the animals that gradually resolved into looks of determination. Everyone turned to their neighbors and an excited buzz soon filled the air as they all began talking. Little as it was, a grim hope had returned to Junk Town.

Twitch and his band helped the atmosphere. Turning to their instruments they began playing a kind of music the animals had never heard before. There were no words to the songs they played, but the music was powerful nonetheless. The animals were soon listening spellbound to music that somehow spoke of their sadness and desperation far better than words could ever do.

Finally stopping for a break several animals applauded the band long and hard. The normally quiet spider Harry the tarantula surprised everyone by being the first to quiz the band about the music.

"What was that, Twitch? I'm pretty sure none of us have ever heard anything like that before."

Twitch smiled at the crowd. "You can thank our parrot friend again. I'm told it's a style called the blues. Rawk likes it and he's had us practicing in secret for a while. It was supposed to be for the next show, but I figured it would be appropriate for tonight."

"That's okay," smiled Rawk. "There are lots of other kinds of music they've never heard that I've got for you to learn for the next show."

"Play us some more!" shouted several members of the crowd.

"Sure," replied the rabbit. "If you're all feeling brave I'll try my new song on you. With everything going on around here I got inspired to try writing my own blues tune. I call it 'The Junk Town Blues'. Let's go, boys!"

The crowd was quickly captivated as they launched into the song. Building slowly, it soon turned into an intense, fast song built around Twitch and his improvised lead guitar sound. The rabbit had clearly been working hard at building his skills and everyone was mesmerized. With a sudden shift in emphasis, Twitch began to sing in a sad voice.

> We're working hard just to survive
> We've all got the Junk Town Blues!
> We need a way to stay alive
> We can't shake the Junk Town Blues!

Finishing with a burst of energy the band ended the song with perfect timing despite no obvious signal being given to stop. The crowd leapt to their feet and roared their approval as one. As the applause finally began to die and the animals were returning to their seats the sound of a commotion in the distance could be heard. As the crowd strained in silence to hear what was going on a chill went down the spine of every animal there as one sound in particular came through. They all knew what the tinkling of bells likely meant.

Several defenders immediately headed in the direction of the sound, only to stop in their tracks in shock. The steady tinkling of the bells came closer and got louder as two wolves with bells around their necks came into view, surrounded by a crowd of border rats holding spears and slingshots at the ready. What was truly puzzling was one of the wolves clutched a white rag in his jaws and was slowly waving it back and forth to ensure everyone saw it.

The group came to a stop in front of Sticks and Twitch. No one spoke for a long moment, until Sticks pointedly looked at the white rag the wolf was now putting on the ground in front of them.

"You are here under a flag of truce, right?" said Sticks.

"Yes. We want to talk," said the other wolf.

"That's a first," snorted Checkers the dog.

"It is," said Sniff the rat, glaring at the dog. "But lets hear what they have to say, shall we? I'm curious to know what they could possibly have to say to us."

"You're the wolf I talked to before, aren't you?" said Sticks, in sudden recognition.

"Yes. You told me it doesn't have to be this way, didn't you?"

"That's right, I did say that. Well, this is interesting. Have you come to join us?"

The wolf doing the talking snorted in mild amusement. "Not likely. You're all going to need every trick you can play and then some to get yourselves out of the pickle you're in now."

Several Junk Town animals stiffened with anger, but Sticks held up a hand to keep them in check. "Okay, look, you didn't come here just to mock us, did you? What do you want?"

"Freedom," replied the wolf. Seeing the puzzled looks on the animals around them the wolf reached up with a paw to clutch at the bells attached to the collar around his neck.

"Let me explain. My name is Nail and this is Winter, my mate. What you need to understand is we've had enough of the pack and we want out. We're running as far away as possible and want to start a new life together. The thing is, you did a real good job with these bells. We haven't been able to figure out how to get them off and I'll be honest, it's been a struggle to survive with them on. That, and as far as the rest of the pack is concerned we're losers and we get treated like dirt because of it. So we're hoping you can get them off us so we can start our life together properly."

Several Junk Town animals looked at each other in stunned surprise. Some were openly scornful, while others just looked puzzled. Rawk's beak dropped open and he slapped his forehead as if he was struck with something he'd forgotten. Sticks glanced at the stunned parrot in curiosity, but knew he had to focus on the wolves so he held up a hand for silence from the crowd.

Despite that Sniff couldn't resist a comment. "Sticks, that's the most ridiculous thing I've ever heard. After everything they've put us through they want mercy?"

"Look, we know this is a stretch," said the wolf. "To prove we're serious we've got some information for you. We know you have little reason to trust us. So we're offering this knowing you might not do what we want."

"No strings attached?" said Sticks.

"No strings. Look, you guys are in big trouble. The next attack is coming real soon. I don't think it'll be tomorrow, but it might be. If it's not tomorrow then it'll be real soon after that. They're throwing everything they have at you."

"Big deal," snorted Sniff. "Like we haven't been expecting an attack. Even a child can see it's coming soon."

"Yeah, but what you don't know is the scale of it. See, Scar has taken over another pack. You guys haven't been the focus lately because we've been fighting on and off with this other pack for territory. Right after that last attempt at you guys a few days ago Scar won a big fight and the survivors of the other pack have joined him. He's got way more wolves than you think now. But that's not all! Scar and his buddy Spike the crow just cut a deal with the seagulls."

"A deal?" said Sticks, a bad feeling stealing over him as he listened to the wolf and several Junk Town animals around him gasped in dismay.

"Oh yeah. See, they've finally figured out how vulnerable you guys are to attacks from the air. I have to admit you've done well until now. Thing is, they want to overwhelm you from the air. They'll wait until you're running around trying to get away from the air attack. Once there's enough confusion on the ground the pack will come in at their leisure and tear you apart. So to get enough birds to take you on they've cut a deal with the seagulls that hang out around the garbage dump, see?"

"I don't believe it," growled Checkers the dog. "The seagulls and the crows are sworn enemies."

"Of course they are," replied the wolf with a savage grin. "And they'll go back to being sworn enemies real fast right after they finish feasting on all of you. Yes, you have a problem. I don't know what you can do about it, but at least you know it's coming now and maybe you got a little time to figure out a defense. So, I don't know if it's of value to know this, but I sure hope so. We'd really like to get these collars off and get out of here. What do you say?"

The watching crowd of animals stared at the wolves for a long moment and then as one turned to look at Sticks. Staring into the distance and clearly deep in thought, Sticks took a few more moments to respond. "I need to consult on this. Relax for a few minutes."

Sticks walked out of earshot of the wolves, gesturing for several of the key Junk Town leaders to follow him. Asking for thoughts from the group a heated discussion quickly resulted. More than a few were deeply suspicious of the two wolves, but everyone had to acknowledge if the information was true the advance knowledge of the plot against them was invaluable.

Sticks listened to them all without saying a word. No one could agree on what to do and when discussion finally faded all eyes turned to him once again. Twitch had been silent throughout the conversation too and sensing the tension among the group he knew it was time to make a decision.

"Well, Sticks, I guess you never expected anything like this when we elected you Mayor," said the rabbit. "This is a tough decision, but I think it's up to you. For me the only real question is whether to trust them. And I'm sorry, but I don't know the answer to that. I do know I trust your judgment and I'll support whatever you decide."

Sticks looked around the rest of the crowd as one by one they all agreed with Twitch and voiced their support. "Well," he said. "Okay, you got it. I know showing forgiveness to a wolf may sound crazy, but like I told him before it doesn't have to be this way. Maybe a little forgiveness will help change things. So let's go see if I'm right."

Turning to go Sticks and Twitch were stopped by Rawk. "Hey guys, so you know, these wolves gave me an idea so I'm going to look into it and see if it can help us. I don't know if it will or not, but I want to try. Time isn't on our side here and it's going to take me a while to get to where I'm going so I'm leaving now. I know you could be in for a fight here and I'd like to help, but this could solve our problems."

Sticks and Twitch looked at each other. "Sure Rawk, we trust you. You've done so much for us already. If you think you've got a solution go for it. We're stick with the plan we've got for now unless you come up with something better."

With a grim smile Rawk pulled the chicken hat off his head and handed it to Sticks. "I'm not feeling frustrated anymore! I'm going to find a way to make this work. Watch for me!" Flapping his wings hard Rawk flew off at top speed.

Returning to where the wolves were still waiting Sticks nodded to Twitch, who in turn nodded to a group of his rabbit engineers. "This will be a good opportunity to test out our new cutting tool. We're pretty sure this'll work for them and it may even work for getting the tag off Stuff's ear."

The eyes of the wolves lit up as the rabbits approached and Sticks looked at them. "So the answer is yes, we do appreciate the information."

The new tool exceeded their hopes and the collars with the bells were soon off both wolves. "Oh, you have no idea how good it feels to get that off," said Nail, as both wolves rubbed their necks with obvious pleasure.

"Okay," said Sticks. "You're free to go and we wish you the best for the future. We don't know what will happen here, but if you won't join us then it would be nice to know we can at least count on you not to attack us if we meet some day in future."

The two wolves looked hard at Sticks and at each other, before Nail finally replied. "Sure, we can agree to that. To be real honest we didn't think you were going to actually do this. So yeah, we agree. For what it's worth, we wish you the best for the future too."

Just as the two wolves turned to walk away a deep, rumbling growl full of menace stopped them in their tracks. Stuff and his mate Honey had arrived and had rushed over as soon as they saw the wolves.

"Stuff!" cried Sticks. "It's okay, they're here under a flag of truce!" As Sticks hastily explained what had happened the two bears gradually calmed down.

Stuff looked at the two wolves with renewed interest. "Well, this is interesting. Never thought I'd see this, but as I've come to learn nothing seems to be impossible for my Junk Town friends. And they even offered to let you stay with them?"

Nail looked back at the huge bear with equal interest. "They did. I have to admit we haven't really taken that idea seriously, though."

"You should. Hey, I'm a big predator and so are you. If I can make them my friends you could too. They could be your new pack. You're wolves, you need a pack, right? Wouldn't it be nice to be in a pack where you were treated with respect?"

The wolf looked uncomfortable. "Well, I guess so. But none of you understand. Once they figure out we're not coming back they'll hunt for us hard and if they catch us it'll be bad, real bad."

"Safety in numbers," said Sticks.

The two wolves looked at each other and muttered low under their breath so no one could hear what they said. "No. Sorry, we have to go. Thank you for this," said Nail. Moments later they were gone.

Everyone was silent for a few moments until Stuff finally spoke up. "You guys do amaze me. If I hadn't seen that for myself I'm not sure I'd have believed it." Turning to Twitch with a start, a sudden look of hope crossed his face. "Say, I see you got their collars off. Does that mean you can get this tag off me?"

The rabbit engineers quickly went to work and to everyone's joy the tag was finally defeated. The bear danced with joy and several animals danced with him.

"Well, that's the first bit of good news we've had in a while. Let's hope it's the just the beginning of more to come!" said Twitch.

Chapter Twelve

The men arrived early the next morning in a small pickup truck. They were the same three men that had dropped off the big machines a few days before, but they seemed in no rush to get started. One of them pulled out a large container of hot coffee and some mugs, pouring some for each of them. The Junk Town animals were already well hidden, waiting to see what would happen.

The wait wasn't long. The woman and the two children drove up and parked beside the small truck. The man in charge of the workers came over and shook hands with the woman as the two children immediately headed for the rear of the trailer to find the animals.

"Hello again," said the man. "The trucks should be here any minute now. So it's confirmed, we haul everything intact to the other junkyard?"

"Yes," she replied. "Everything except this old trailer and the barn with all the junk out back. I'm hoping you can haul that stuff all away to the garbage dump, as the other junkyard doesn't want it." A sudden look of concern crossed her face as she continued. 'Will your equipment be enough to deal with the old buildings?"

"This?" laughed the man. "The bulldozer will have this flattened in no time. Ah, here they come."

A distant steady rumble of sound grew steadily louder from the direction of the road. A line of big dump trucks finally came into view, stopping just outside the entrance to Junk Town. A few of the truck drivers came over to get instructions from the man in charge and then returned to their vehicles. The man then nodded to the two men who finished their coffee and went toward the two machines.

By this time the children had found the animals and a hurried conference began. "We're sorry!" wailed the girl as soon as she saw them. 'We tried to convince Mom to stop this, but she just won't listen. She doesn't believe us."

"It's okay," said Twitch. "We know you tried. Well, we still have some time here anyway."

"Time?" cried the boy. "How can that be? They're about to haul everything away and tear your home apart."

Twitch smiled. "Well, they may end up doing all that sooner or later, but it won't be today. Watch."

The first man to try starting his machine was the bulldozer driver. When the machine failed to start a puzzled look stole over his face. Looking over at the man in charge for help he began fiddling with the starter for the engine, but continued to get no response at all. The other man had meanwhile now reached the front-end loader and tried starting it, only to get the same result. He looked over at the man on the bulldozer and shrugged. Turning, he looked at the man in charge and held out his arms, palms up, to show he had no idea what was going on.

The leader of the men rushed over to the machines and all three held a hurried conference together. Soon the hatch covering the engine to the bulldozer was open and all three were peering inside. With a start all three suddenly stepped back, looking at each other. One of them ran over to the other machine, opening the hatch covering that engine too. He peered in for a few moments, then turned and nodded grimly to their leader.

The two workers did a thorough inspection of the inside of both machines while their leader made a call on his cell phone. Eventually the three men closed the engine covers and walked over to where the woman was standing. By this time a few of the truck drivers were also on their way over to join the group, wondering why nothing was happening.

"What's going on, guys?" asked the woman.

"Uh, well, you may not believe this, but it looks like we won't be able to get started until tomorrow," replied the leader, as several of the truck drivers groaned. "Both machines have been disabled. The wiring has been cut in several places. We're going to have to replace pretty much all of the wire cabling in them. I think I can get replacements by the end of the day today, but the installation of it all will have to wait till tomorrow."

"What do you mean, the wires have been cut?" said the woman, a look of shock on her face. "Who would cut the wires? Why would anyone do that?"

"Uh, well, I should be clearer. I said 'cut', but the wires have actually been chewed through."

"Chewed?"

"Well, that's what it looks like. They aren't clean cuts. You can see the marks of their teeth. Have you seen any rabbits around here by any chance?"

"Rabbits?" said the woman, as she heard her children laughing in the distance. "Ah, no, I haven't, but my children, wherever they are, did mention to me they had seen some in the area."

"Ah, well, they would be the likely culprits. I haven't seen this before myself, but I 've heard of it. For whatever reason, these silly rabbits like to chew the wiring. Sorry about this, but we're done for today. We'll be back first thing tomorrow to make some repairs and get going."

"But..." said the woman, still trying to grasp what had happened. "This is going to cost more, isn't it?"

"Uh, well, yeah. We'll have to charge you something, I should think. I'll talk to the owners back in town. Maybe we can just charge you an hour or two of everyone's time. Sorry."

"Are you sure you can get back on track tomorrow? I've got a tight deadline to get this junk off the property otherwise the deal won't go through with the developer," said the woman, looking very worried.

The man shrugged. "If I can get the wiring I need, which I'm real sure I can, it'll take the boys here maybe a couple of hours tomorrow morning to do the installation. We'll try and get here a little early and I'll call for the dump trucks when I'm sure we're on track. We'll do our best. Right, lets get going, boys." Turning away, he issued a series of orders to the men. Returning to their trucks, they got in and drove away.

The woman remained where she was for a few moments, groaning and holding her head in her hands. Walking over to the machines she lifted the engine cover on one and peered inside.

The watching children and animals all looked at each other. "What do you think?" said the girl. "Will she listen now?"

The boy shrugged. "I guess we better go find out."

"Before you go you need to know what's been happening here," said Sticks. Looks of concern soon appeared on the children's faces as Sticks began filling them in on what had been learned from the two wolves.

"So you see, it's vital you get the location of the other junkyard for us," concluded Sticks. "The rabbits stopped the machines once, but when the men put in the new wiring there won't be any way to stop them. We have nowhere else to go. Please?"

The children were horrified. "We'll do the best we can," said Sarah, grasping her brother's arm as they both turned and ran to their mother.

The woman was just closing the engine cover on the front-end loader as the children ran up. They stopped short, seeing the anger on her face. She vented it on the machine, slamming the cover down hard to close it. Turning, she saw the children and knew she had to master herself.

"Mom? Are you okay?" asked the girl.

The woman took a few moments to reply. "No. No, I'm not okay. Sorry, kids, it's not you. I'm just frustrated and scared. Look, I'll be honest with you. We need to get this junk out of here and the sale to the developer to go through. If it doesn't we'll be ruined. We don't have the money to pay for everything."

"Mom, the animals were just trying to protect their home. They didn't want to cause us problems."

"Well, that may be, but they have. Come on, let's go."

"Mom, we need to do something for the animals, don't we? They're taking all the junk to another junkyard, right? Where is it? We can tell the animals and they can maybe go there," said the boy.

The woman was already on her way back to the car. "Huh? Where is the other junkyard? Oh, it's way over on the far side of the city." She waved a hand vaguely in the direction of the city as she reached the car.

The children ran to catch up. "Mom?" said the girl. "Can we help the animals get there?"

The woman stopped herself from getting in the car, an exasperated look on her face. "Look, I love you both for caring, but what happens to a few rabbits isn't our problem."

"But Mom! There are all kinds of animals here. They used to be pets and they have nowhere to go."

The woman groaned in frustration. "Kids, a few animals that can't find a way to live in the forest are the least of our problems! The developer taking over this place will have to deal with them. Are there no animal shelters they could go to? Are there no zoos? Of course there are! It's not our problem. Get in the car, please."

The children groaned, worried and frustrated that they hadn't succeeded. Looking over to where they knew the Junk Town animals were hiding they could only offer a resigned shrug.

As they did, a squawk of laughter came from above. The children and the animals turned as one to look for the source, knowing instinctively there was something different about the sound.

They were right. Three large seagulls were sitting on the roof of the old trailer and had clearly been watching everything that happened with amusement. Strutting about for a few moments they continued laughing until as one they lifted into the air and flew off in the direction of the dump.

The children's mother called again, using a sharper tone of voice this time, but only the boy obeyed.

"We're sorry!" called the girl as she ran over to where she knew the animals were hiding. "All we could find out is the other junkyard is somewhere on the far side of the city. We'll try and get better information for you tomorrow."

Running back to her now angry mother the girl climbed into the car. As they drove away the Junk Town animals emerged from hiding and gathered in a worried group.

"What do you think, Twitch?" said Sticks. "It looks like our wolf friends were right. Is there any way we can leave here today?"

The rabbit's face was grim. "They're working as fast as they can, but they won't have our little wagons ready until late tonight. Sure, we could leave now, but we wouldn't be able to take anywhere near enough supplies to defend ourselves and keep us fed along the way. And where exactly would we go? All we have right now is this vague idea it's on the other side of the city. We all know the predators will be able to track us. I don't know, Sticks. If we really must leave here I'd rather leave as prepared as possible to defend ourselves."

Sticks sighed, as did several other animals. "Yeah, I already knew that was the answer. I had to ask anyway. Right, has anyone seen Rawk today?"

Everyone looked around and several animals just shook their heads, so Sticks continued. "Huh, I guess there's no hope for us there. Well, everyone, it looks like this is our last day in Junk Town. Lets hope the children bring something with them tomorrow to give us a clearer sense of where the other junkyard is. Let's be ready to leave as soon as we have it. It's early to bed tonight, too, for everyone. Are we agreed?"

The watching animals were grim, but determined. Sticks issued a series of orders for them to work on what seemed an impossible list of things to do. Accepting their orders with nods of agreement the Junk Town animals went their separate ways.

Turning to Twitch, Sticks held him back. "Twitch, I think we may need a little help tomorrow. The wolves said it would be real soon and I think those gulls we saw were scouts. What do you think?"

Twitch nodded. "I agree. I'll get some messages sent out."

Chapter Thirteen

Although the days were now slowly getting shorter once again it was still an early summer dawn the next morning. The animals had worked hard the day before and slept deeply that night. They felt refreshed, but there was a tension in the air from knowing they were heading into an unknown future this day.

The future didn't keep them waiting long. As promised the same three men from the day before drove into Junk Town early to do repairs to the damaged machines. A little trailer pulled behind the truck was filled with several large bales of wiring. Yawning, they got out and began drinking coffee from their mugs like the day before. The animals had immediately gone into hiding as soon as they arrived.

Finishing their coffees the men set to work. Pulling out several tools and long lengths of coated wires they were soon busy working on both machines. The damaged wiring came free with their determined efforts and a large pile soon began to grow. With their heads buried deep in the machines they had no idea the biggest attack the Junk Town animals had ever faced was underway.

The defenders knew it had started, though. The skies above them filled with birds coming from several directions and, as predicted by the two wolves, there were indeed a host of seagulls joining the crows.

Sticks and Twitch groaned when they saw the attack coming. "It was too much to hope they would hold off just a little longer, wasn't it?" said the rabbit.

But the defenders were also as ready as they were ever going to be for it. As the air filled with squawking crows and screeching seagulls with vicious, sharp yellow beaks a storm of rocks flew up to greet them. Knowing the strategy of the birds was to break the Junk Town defenses and sow confusion on the ground helped. Most of the stubborn defenders had retreated to the castles strategically placed throughout Junk Town, but not all.

The Junk Town rats led by Sniff along with a few volunteers from other animal groups were a mobile attack group. Being able to move quickly from one spot to another meant they could circle around behind birds trying to attack the castles and shoot at them, catching them with deliberate crossfire.

"Come and get it, you flying turkeys!" screamed Sniff. "You're not having us today!"

A stalemate soon developed. As predicted, there were plenty of birds, but there was no coordination to their attack. Sniff and his mobile group of attackers soon began to turn the tide as one by one birds were brought down by slingshots and the sticks of the defenders. Within moments a full dozen of the attackers were stretched out unconscious on the ground. Those that were still conscious after they fell from the sky didn't stay that way long as Sniff and his followers quickly swarmed the dazed birds and pounded them into submission.

The commotion was loud enough to raise the curiosity of the men, however. "What's all that racket behind the trailer about, boss?" asked one of the workers.

"I have no idea," he replied, a look of concern on his face. "It sounds like something bad is going on over there. Get something to arm yourself with just in case and follow me." The two workers picked up a heavy tool each while their leader grabbed a big stick lying on the ground nearby.

Rounding the corner of the trailer the three men stumbled to a halt in shock. "Boss, what's going on here?" asked one of the workers. "I... Whoa, did you see that? Those rats just used slingshots to shoot at that bird! Am I seeing things?"

The human leader was still stunned, trying to take it all in, and had no reply. And then, it was too late.

Scar couldn't keep his wolves at bay any longer. "Remember, the spider is mine! I have a score to settle with him!"

Turning them loose, he watched them go and began to stroll towards the battle with a smile. Scar had learned from his last big fight with the Junk Town defenders. This time, he would let others do the dirty work until he was ready to personally get involved.

The howls of the rampaging wolves were truly frightening. They came from all directions and even more frightening, there seemed too many to count. Several fell prey to traps the crows hadn't spied out for them, but it seemed to make little difference to the numbers attacking Junk Town. The three men were shocked to find themselves in the middle of a desperate battle and the wolves weren't being fussy about who they faced. The desire for a fight was upon them and this time there were no frightening machines roaring to scare them off.

Several wolves quickly surrounded the three men, while even more streamed past to attack Junk Town. All the men could do was stand with their backs to each other in fright. The wolves immediately began lunging from all different directions to try and catch them off guard. They paid for it, though, as the men quickly realized they were fighting for their lives and responded accordingly. Soon enough two wolves had to pull back from the fight with badly bruised snouts from being struck by the men. The wolves had made it through to wound one of the men, though. The injured man had torn pants and was bleeding just above his knee from the jaws of a large, aggressive wolf.

The three humans being involved in the fight was a development the defenders hadn't expected. However, the stalemate between the wolves and the three men was the least of the concerns the Junk Town animals faced. Seeing the wolves had joined the fight Sticks signaled to Twitch and the other Junk Town leaders the time had come to spring a few surprises on their foes.

"Let them have it! For Junk Town!" cried the stick bug.

"Junk Town!" screamed a host of voices in response.

The predators were taken aback for a moment, knowing their foes ability to throw something unexpected at them. And they did.

The three new castles the rabbits had built over the course of the winter held surprises. A swarm of animals climbed into the towers and began pulling panels off the sides, revealing huge slingshots that could swivel in all directions. An ingenious pulley system brought fresh ammunition up to the shooters on the slingshot platform at the top. Soon enough huge rocks were flying all directions as the frustrated wolves began milling about. They couldn't get at the slingshots and the deadly hail of rocks had them dodging for cover.

That wasn't the only little surprise Twitch had in store for them. One of the wolves near the humans unexpectedly reeled from a rock hammered into the back of his head. He was shocked, as he had looked behind him only a few seconds before and knew there were no foes there. What he didn't know was the rabbit engineers had been busy underground, too. As he searched for the source the surprise prepared by the defenders became clear.

As the shocked wolf watched a rabbit with a slingshot suddenly popped up and took a shot at another unsuspecting wolf, hitting him in the back of the head and stunning him too. As soon as the missile was fired the rabbit disappeared from view. Moments later, three more rabbits appeared in different spots and did exactly the same thing.

Rushing over to where the rabbit had disappeared the wolf finally understood what was happening. A hole in the ground was cleverly hidden in the middle of a clump of tall grass so no one would realize it was there.

"Tunnels!" he howled, warning his mates. "They've got tunnels everywhere! Watch... Oww!" Stumbling back the wolf crashed to the ground unconscious. A large rock had come flying from the hole the moment he showed his face and whacked him square on the forehead.

The defenses were holding, but the sheer numbers of attackers was beyond even the wildest estimates of Sticks and Twitch. Both were worried, knowing that the numbers would overwhelm the Junk Town animals eventually.

The messages for help sent the night before paid off, though. A storm of acorns shot from little slingshots filled the air and hammered the attacking birds as a large group of forest squirrels in the trees joined the battle. Another storm of smaller forest birds swooped in after the Spike the crow leader, surrounding him in a swirling mass of feathers. At close quarters the speedy little birds could surround and swarm the much larger crows and gulls, rushing in to peck at them.

Sniff and his mobile attack group were in trouble though. He had misjudged just how many attackers there were and had not sought shelter fast enough. The wolves had cut off the nearest path to safety and it was only a matter of time before they were overwhelmed.

Windy and her uncle Twiggs were part of the group. Desperately trying to win a path through the two were themselves cut off and surrounded. Sticks was busy directing the fire of defenders from one of the castles, but he was also

trying to keep an eye on the overall battle. Sticks
went cold with fear for Windy when he saw what
was happening.

"Windy! I'm coming! Hold on!" In
desperation he charged out from the safety of the
castle in a headlong charge, despite knowing there
was no way he could get there in time. The animals
left behind looked at each other with questioning
looks, before they rushed as one to follow Sticks.
"Junk Town!" they screamed, bowling the startled
wolves in their path to the side.

But it wasn't Sticks that saved the day. Two
wolves crashed into the ring of attackers from
behind, creating a path to safety just as the stick
bugs were about to be overwhelmed. "Back off,"
snarled Nail, with Winter prowling at his side.

The attacking wolves were stunned at being
attacked by one of their own kind, but only for a
moment. "Traitors!" screamed one of the larger
attackers as he and Nail smashed into each other.
The distraction was enough to save the two
desperate stick bugs. A wave of defenders swept
the rest of the attacking wolves back as Nail won
the battle with his foe, who backed away bleeding
in several places. As they met up they joined Sniff
and his now much larger group of roving fighters in
a formidable bunch.

An angry roar cut the air as Stuff and his
mate Honey joined the battle. The wolves were
dismayed, but didn't back down. Knowing what
the roar meant, Scar called up his reserves. Several
wolves that had not been able to join in due to the
sheer numbers of attackers immediately surrounded
the two angry bears.

Scar strolled over to the crowd surrounding the two bears and stood on the fringe. "Stupid bears!" he said, mocking their efforts. "You won't get your way this time. I've got so many wolves here even you can't take them all on. And sooner or later you're going to get tired. When you do, you'll both end up part of the feast we're going to have for the next few nights!"

"Big talk, wolf," growled Stuff. "But I don't think you've got everything as under control as you think? Right, Buster?"

Scar looked puzzled, wondering whom the bear was talking to. A heavy weight landing with jarring force on the back of Scar's head and neck gave him the answer. "Hi, Scar, nice to meet you!" chittered the monkey.

Scar did his best for a few moments to try and shake the monkey off, but Buster was tenacious and held on tight. That wasn't what sent a chill down the wolf's spine, however.

"I've been waiting for you, Scar," said a different voice, coming from right beside the wolf's ear. Scar knew who the voice belonged to and shook his head violently, but he couldn't do it for long. Buster's passenger, Harry the tarantula, was just as tenacious as the monkey in holding on.

Crawling over the top of the wolf's head and onto his snout, Harry turned and glared hard into the eyes of the desperate wolf. Scar tried to bat him off his nose, but the spider took the blow and simply grinned at the cross-eyed wolf staring back in fear. Scar knew what was coming.

"Well, it seems you're a slow learner, Scar," said the spider. "We're just going to have to repeat the lesson!" The spider grinned as he sank his fangs deep into the wolf's sensitive nose. Howling in pain, Scar rolled on the ground holding a paw to his throbbing nose as both Harry and Buster jumped off him.

The fight with the humans on the other side of the clearing was meanwhile still a desperate battle. The human leader, though, had been shocked to a new level of desperation seeing the two bears arrive. Not realizing the bears were no threat to him the man spurred himself to break through the ring of attackers and run for his truck.

"Keep them occupied!" he screamed to his two followers. "I'm getting help!"

The two men now standing back-to-back fighting off the wolves had no time or thought to reply as the sight of over two dozen eagles crashing hard into the attacking birds and wolves was enough to make their jaws drop open in stunned surprise. The birds screeched in anger as they attacked, adding to the chaos of the scene. The battle grew to a fever pitch and who would taste victory was impossible to predict.

The harsh roar from both barrels of a double-barreled shotgun ripped the air and struck fear into the heart of every animal present. Freezing them in their tracks, they turned as one to look for the source. As they did, the sound of a vehicle pulling into Junk Town came from behind the old trailer.

Rushing back to his truck, the human leader had pulled out the shotgun he knew was there and returned to the fight, discharging both barrels into the air. The man glared about as he calmly reloaded the shotgun from an ammunition belt strung around his shoulder, snapping the gun closed in readiness.

"Right," said the man. "I've had enough of this. Who wants it first?"

As he spoke the woman and her children came around the corner of the trailer and stumbled to a halt. Her jaw dropped open as she took in the host of animals staring back and at the man holding the gun. She finally settled her gaze on the man, giving him a despairing, pleading look as her shoulders slumped.

"What is going on here?! Please tell me I'm seeing things."

"I sure wish I knew," said the man.

"And the machines aren't repaired yet?"

"Nope. Been a little busy here."

The woman groaned, holding her head in despair, as the predators finally stirred.

Knowing it was over the attacking wolves began stumbling over each other in their desperation to get away. The host of crows and gulls did the same, flapping in frantic haste to find a clear path to freedom. Stuff and his mate were both wary of humans with guns, so they too quickly slipped away into the forest.

As the rush to get away continued the sound of yet another vehicle entering Junk Town came from behind the trailer. A door slammed shut and moments later a man with graying hair no one had seen before walked around the corner of the trailer. Sitting on his shoulder was Rawk the parrot. The two joined the little group of humans and stopped, looking around with curiosity at the watching animals and especially at the human with the gun.

"Hey, I'm back!" said Rawk, fluffing his feathers up. "Did you all miss me? Say, did I miss anything important while I was gone?"

Chapter Fourteen

The Junk Town animals were relieved the fight was over. Many simply collapsed where they were, exhausted from the battle. Several had little cuts and bruises that were quickly examined while a wary eye was kept on the humans. Many had thoughts of hiding, but seeing Sticks and Twitch standing fast to await developments gave them courage to do so too. As they thought about it, they realized there was little point in hiding anymore.

The woman was almost in tears as she composed herself and spoke to the leader of the workers. "Please, I don't know what's going on here, but I do know I need you to get this job on track. I'll be ruined if this doesn't work."

"Mom," said the little girl. "We tried to tell you. These are the animals that have been abandoned. They're just trying to survive. They live here." She paused a moment to give the adults a desperate, pleading look. "We've got to do something to help them."

The leader of the workers looked at the children with a sudden light of understanding and then looked around at the crowd of animals watching from a wary distance. Shaking his head as if trying to wake from a strange dream, the man glanced over at his men. "Guys, head for the truck. There's a first aid kit there you can use to get fixed up. I'll be with you in a minute."

Turning, he looked back at the woman, with a momentary curious look at the old man standing with Rawk on his shoulder. "Right, well,

I'm not sure what that was all about, but I'll let you figure that out. In case you didn't notice, those were wolves and bears running around here. I'm going to get back to work and we'll get this going for you, don't worry."

Pausing for a moment before leaving, he patted the shotgun in his arms. "I'll be keeping this real close at hand. Give a shout if those wolves or bears come back." With a final curious look around the man shrugged and walked away.

The remaining adults watched him leave and then turned to each other. "Uh, hello?" said the woman. "And you are..."

"Willy, nice to meet you. I gather you're the owner of Junk Town?"

"Well, yes, but hopefully not much longer. I... I'm sorry, but I have to ask. Why do you have your parrot on your shoulder?"

"Oh, him? He's not my parrot." Seeing her puzzled look, the man smiled. "I'm told he's one of the animals that lives here."

"That's right," said the children in unison. "His name is Rawk."

The woman just groaned and put a hand to her forehead. "Okay, look, so what can I do for you?"

"Well, my parrot friend here told me about these animals and that they might need a new home. I thought I'd come and check it out, because I can maybe help."

The children's faces lit with joy. "Oh, Mister Willy, that would be wonderful!" Small, hopeful looks appeared on the faces of the watching Junk Town animals too.

"Help?" said the woman.

"Maybe I could help with a little background?" said Rawk. "We know you've sold Junk Town and there's no provision made for us to stay here. We've been hoping to find a new junkyard for a home, but it finally dawned on me that maybe there was another alternative. So I talked to Willy here and he agrees."

Staring hard for a long moment at Rawk the woman finally brushed a hand across her face. "I'm actually understanding what this bird is saying. This place is starting to get to me."

Holding up a hand, she signaled she wanted to continue. "Okay, that's fine. I'm just going to run with this crazy dream. I guess I should have been paying more attention to what my kids are telling me. So tell us, how can you help?"

"Why, I can give them a new home if they want it."

"All of these animals? There seems to be rather a lot of them. What about all these eagles?" asked the woman, waving at the flock of eagles perched high in the trees watching what was happening.

"Ah, the eagles aren't a problem. They already live with me. They just flew here because Rawk asked them to come and help if they could."

"So where do you live, Mister Willy?" asked the boy.

"Way over there," said the man, pointing away from the city towards the mountains in the distance.

"How big is your place? Is there enough room for all of them?"

"Oh, sure," replied the man with a dismissive wave. "I should clarify, though, this isn't actually my place." Seeing more puzzled looks the man just smiled. "See, I live in a school. It's actually called The Wilderness School. I work there. School's out now for the summer, but when school is in they bring kids from the city out to the school. The idea is kids will learn a lot more seeing plants and animals and rocks and things out in the wild than they would sitting in a stale old classroom in the city. The teachers come out with them, of course, and they stay overnight for a couple of days. Once they're gone a new group comes in. We have a few animals there already, but we could always use more."

"Wow," said the boy. "That sounds neat. So the kids get to play while they're at the school?"

"Well, maybe a little," laughed the man. "But the teachers make them work, just like they were back in the city. The only difference is school is outside every day, all day, unless the weather is really bad."

The children looked at each other and then back at their mother. "That sounds like my kind of school, Mom. Can we go there?" asked the girl.

Rawk leapt off the man's shoulder and flew over to the watching crowd of animals as the woman reminded the children they would be flying home once Junk Town was sold. Landing in the middle of the animals Rawk grinned and looked around.

"I have no idea why this didn't occur to me earlier. Remember our eagle friends that helped us last year? They live at the Wilderness School now with all these other eagles and more. Plenty of salmon to eat in the river! So what do you think?"

"Uhh, Rawk, where would we live there?" asked Twitch. "Is there material we can use to build homes?"

"Sure! The human has a big workshop there. There's lots of wood and material. There's lots of room, too. The school has a real big piece of cleared land. There are lots of buildings on the site that the teachers and the kids stay in."

The hopeful looks grew on hearing this, but when he finished talking the animals looked as one to Sticks.

"Ah, Rawk, just a couple of questions. How far away is this place?"

"Actually, it's quite a ways from here. I had to fly for over a day full speed just to get there. It's far enough that I don't think Scar and his buddies will want to travel all that way just to get us, if that's what you're wondering."

"Yes, it was. Okay, what about our wolf friends here?" Turning, Sticks pointed to the two wolves hiding almost out of sight behind one of the Junk Town castles. Only their faces could be seen as they peered around a corner, watching events unfold.

"See, they helped us in the fight. They came back when they didn't have to. Apparently Stuff talked them into it. The thing is, they can't leave here now. They're trapped. Scar and his pack know they're here now. I'm quite sure there's a ring of wolves hiding around Junk Town just waiting for them. They'll be torn apart if they leave here."

"Hmm, wolves," said Rawk, a thoughtful look on his face. "That could be a problem if they want to stay with us at the School. I mean, we know they won't hurt us, but I'm not sure the humans will understand."

"Can we maybe help them get out? Maybe they can travel with us? Once we get to the School they should be far enough away they can make a new home for themselves safely in the forest."

"Sure, I should be able to get the human to help with that. So what other questions do you have?"

"Uh, well, none. I just need to know the animals want to give this a try. Well, everyone?"

Sticks looked around, seeing only hope and nods of agreement. "Okay, I guess that's your answer." Turning, Sticks found Twitch at his side. "Twitch, we'll have to get a message out to our friends in the forest and to Stuff to let them know what's happening." As Twitch nodded, Sticks turned back to the parrot. "I don't know how we can thank you, Rawk. You've come through for us again."

Rawk grinned and did a little dance on the spot. "I'll make sure Stuff knows where you've gone. You won't regret this, everyone. It's a beautiful spot. Oh, hey, I forgot to tell you the best part!"

"What?" said Sticks.

"The school has a big gym with a stage! It even has proper spotlights and a curtain. I can hardly wait for my first show!"

***

The old human was surprised to see the two wolves and reluctant at first to bring them. Gradually, though, he got over his initial shock at seeing them and as Rawk patiently explained their role he finally agreed to help.

One problem remained as no one had fully thought through how they would all get to The Wilderness School safely. Knowing there was a host of frustrated, angry enemies waiting for the humans to leave made the thought of walking to the school unpleasant.

Part of the solution was Willy had fortunately brought a pick up truck with him. Riding in the back would be uncomfortable, but the animals could all get there safely and a lot faster than if they'd had to walk. The problem was they couldn't all fit in his truck. The woman finally agreed, after prodding from her children, to take as many animals as she could in her car. However, as they stood looking at the two vehicles they realized there still wasn't enough room.

The leader of the workers came to the rescue. They'd finally rewired the two machines and the roars of their engines coming to life confirmed success. As the dump trucks began lining up outside Junk Town he gave orders to his men and then joined the crowd for an explanation of what was happening.

"Well, sure, I'll help if that's what it takes to keep this job on track. I can take the rest of these animals in my truck. The trailer I brought to haul all the wire today will help do the job too. The guys know what they're doing now so I can leave." Glaring hard at the two wolves as they gingerly walked past him to climb into the old man's truck, he looked over at the Willy. "You're really taking these wolves with you?"

Willy just shrugged. "I know. This seems a little strange doesn't it?"

"Huh," replied the man. "This whole thing is strange. Whatever, let's go."

As the last of the Junk Town animals climbed into the vehicles the bulldozer was already doing its work. The huge machine didn't even slow as it crashed into the old humans trailer and crumpled it as if it had been made of toothpicks. Continuing on the blade of the machine began shoving the former homes of the animals into a big pile with ease.

Several animals watching had tears in their eyes. Windy was crying too as she came to stand beside Sticks. He put an arm around her and did his best to keep a strong face for those around him.

"We weren't here for long, but I'm going to miss this place," she cried. "It's where we met. We've been happy here."

"I know," said Sticks. "But we don't have any choice, do we? We'll just have to find a way to make our new home just as good."

***

The drive to the school was long and, as expected, very uncomfortable. The reward was what awaited them, though. As the animals climbed out of the vehicles their weariness left them.

The mountains were much closer now and the air was much cooler. The clean, fresh scent of pine trees was everywhere. The school was indeed big, with plenty of cleared land dotted with trees and paths everywhere. A river could be seen in the distance. The music of its water rushing down from the mountains on its way to the ocean was wonderful. Warm sunlight glittered off its surface.

The smiles on the faces of the animals and the tears in the eyes of many told Sticks all he needed to know. Pulling Windy close, he felt the strain of the last days in Junk Town melt away.

"Welcome to The Wilderness School everyone," said Willy.

The End

Afterword

I have a couple of things I'd like you to
know and understand.

In ancient Greece people writing plays to
perform for the public would sometimes find
themselves painted into a corner because of the
complicated plots they wrote. With no logical way
out they would turn to a device called a 'deus ex
machina'. This literally means 'god from a
machine'. The playwright would have an actor
appear as one of the Greek 'gods' using a machine
such as a crane suspending the 'god' in the sky
above the other actors. Another way would be to
have a machine lift the 'god' into view from
beneath the stage. The 'god' would then give
directions to the actors resolving the impossibly
complicated situation and the play could continue.

In modern times 'deus ex machina' has
generally come to refer to a plot development so
ridiculous that its impossible for the audience to
believe it could happen. Using a 'deus ex machina'
is usually considered the sign of a lazy, uninspired
writer and one should avoid doing so unless you
have a very, very good reason.

I mention all of this because I'm concerned
some of you may be thinking I was using a 'deus ex
machina' when I introduced the idea of the Junk
Town animals moving to a children's school in the
middle of the forest. Now, I know what you're
thinking. This is after all a fantasy novel, so where's
the problem?

Yes, it is a fantasy novel, but aside from
using stick bugs and engineer rabbits that can do

and build just about anything and having animals that can talk to each other and to certain humans, I have tried to otherwise ground the stick bug stories in realism.

So yes, there really is a school that children can and do go to out in the forest which inspired me to include this element in these stories. One of the School Districts in the city where I live actually has a school in the forest outside the city called The Outdoor School. Children of all ages visit the school periodically throughout the school year and learn about nature in the best possible way.

My point, therefore, is having the abandoned animals find a new home in a school in the middle of the wilderness is not a 'deus ex machina'. It's very true I have my share of lazy moments, but on this particular point I am not guilty.

I have one more thing to touch on. I simply couldn't resist a little tribute to the 1951 movie 'A Christmas Carol' and the story it was based on of the same name by the brilliant author Charles Dickens. If you've never seen this wonderful movie and Alastair Sim's excellent portrayal of the miser Ebenezer Scrooge, well, be assured you will enjoy watching it.

At one point in the story Scrooge is asked to make a donation to a fund to help the poor. Being a miser who thought the taxes he pays were enough to do the job, he responded with the classic lines "Are there no prisons? Are there no workhouses?" In The Junk Town Blues the woman responds to her children's pleas to help the soon to be displaced animals with "Are there no zoos? Are there no animal shelters?"

Is it fair to make this connection, you ask? I'm not a big fan of zoos or aquariums, but I acknowledge they do good work with education and offering support to injured animals that can no longer be released into the wild. Animal shelters of course offer obvious support to animals in need. Bottom line, though, I don't think animals in zoos and animal shelters really want to be there any more than humans want to be in prisons or in workhouses for the poor.

I hope you enjoyed The Junk Town Blues. And what will the future hold for the abandoned animals? 'Stick Bugs In School' will tell that final piece of their story.

Stick Bugs In School

With Junk Town a demolished ruin and soon to be a construction site, the abandoned animals had little choice but to try making a new home at The Wilderness School.

Will it be all they hope? How will they fit in at Wilderness School anyway? And are they finally rid of the predators? Find out in the third and final book of the stick bug stories series.

'Stick Bugs In School' will be available spring 2015.

Made in the USA
Charleston, SC
25 April 2014